THE LIBERATION OF FOLKS BELL

Peyton Eli Bell III

authorHOUSE®

AuthorHouse™
1663 Liberty Drive
Bloomington, IN 47403
www.authorhouse.com
Phone: 1-800-839-8640

Published by AuthorHouse 2/27/2012

ISBN: 978-1-4634-1703-1 (sc)
ISBN: 978-1-4634-1701-7 (e)

Library of Congress Control Number: 2011910021

Any people depicted in stock imagery provided by Thinkstock are models, and such images are being used for illustrative purposes only. Certain stock imagery © Thinkstock.

This book is printed on acid-free paper.

CONTENTS

CHAPTER 1

The septa bus slowed to a stop on the busy street corner. A very astute looking woman wearing a chic dress and a pearl necklace stepped off the bus. Behind her, a very handsome man, well dressed in gray dress pants and a matching gray fedora, casually strolled down the steps. He would come to be known as one of the most diabolical scientists the world had ever had the misfortune of meeting: RAUL TESTO! Testo took a look around, swiped a newspaper from a newsstand and gently leaned against the wall of The National Trust Bank all in one cool motion. From behind his newspaper, Testo eyed the crowd to see if anyone noticed him. He then planted a small black box shaped device against the wall and pressed one of its two buttons. He moved towards the door of the bank and several seconds later all hell broke loose! The buildings and the ground immediately started to rumble and shake; car alarms started wailing. As people ran, a large piece of a building fell and crushed a man running for cover. All evidence pointed to a massive earthquake. But in Philadelphia?!

In the chaos that ensued, Testo made his way into The National Trust Bank, and headed down to the basement. He came to a keypad and punched in a code that opened a secret wall to a room that was spotless, having only a small black leather chaise and file cabinets built into the wall. Each file cabinet had six small black dots on them. Testo pulled a small metal needle from his pocket and began touching the black dots with the needle in different sequences. One by one each file drawer popped open. Testo then started taking specific papers from certain drawers. He placed the papers in a satchel and made his way back up to the first floor of the bank and out the door.

Outside, the chaos continued. Testo rounded the corner in smooth steps laughing to himself as people dashed about in terror as the world crumbled under their feet. Testo then pushed the second button on the black box device, and just like that the earth stopped shaking. However, this seemed to panic the people even more. By now they'd had time to get their thoughts together to assess this crazy development.

Testo made his way up the street without anyone noticing him. He rounded a corner as a long black 1983 Cadillac eased up beside him and Raul Testo calmly entered. The Cadillac pulled off into the chaotic day. < end of sample>

The sign above the door to the observatory simply read "BELIEVE IN YOURSELF", but it seemed to bother the hell out of Folks Bell. The sign, hung there years earlier by another astronomer, was intended to always keep the focus of future astronomers. Folks loved looking at the stars. Unlike most astronomers who had thousands of intricate theories on space and the stars, Folks didn't! He just enjoyed the beauty of nature's creation. He could look at the stars for hours, which he often did as a child. The knock at the door broke his gaze and concentration. Dr. Sala C. Bright entered the room of the main observatory. Dr. Bright was a tall, slim, brown skinned man closing in on sixty, but whose eyes were as bright as any young man. Dr. Bright loved Folks like a son. He was very aware of the man's uncanny knowledge about space, but strangely not amazed by that fact. Folks was his best student ,and now co- worker. The observatory housed six scientists, and at least two were mandated to be at the observatory at all times. The five scientist were all hand picked by Dr. Bright for their skills and knowledge. Dr. Bright used to work at Area 51, Unit C on sector 9, but never would he talk about this to anyone. His students would always try slick ways of questioning him about his experiences at Area 51, to which he would only reply it was too boring to talk about. "Evening Folks" Dr. Bright said to Folks Bell.

"Dr. Bright, good evening," Folks said. The younger man was great at telling people's emotions and he could tell that something was bothering Dr. Bright. " Is everything ok, Dr. Bright?" he asked.

Just then the Doctor's cell phone rang and he walked into another room to answer it. A few minutes later Dr. Bright came rushing out of the room. "Folks, take a ride with me," he demanded.

"A ride?! Where? Who is going watch the observatory?" Folks asked.

"I-I-have to see a friend. Folks it's an emergency!" stated Dr. Bright.

Is everything ok? What's wrong?" Folks asked as he grabbed his jacket.

Dr. Bright gave Folks a look, and Folks knew to grab the car keys and follow him! In the parking lot, Folks was still wondering what was going on as he got into the driver's seat of his 2005 Ford Taurus and looked at Dr. Bright.

The older man demanded that Folks drive him to a home in Bala Cynwyd, so they set out. A half hour later, they pulled into a driveway of a huge expensive looking house. Dr. Bright rushed from the car to the back door of the house. Folks followed closely behind wondering still what might be happening. Inside, an Asian man who had to be at least seventy-five years old, eagerly greeted them. Although Folks had never seen this man before, the old man looked at Folks as if he had known him a long time. "Sala, he looks very strong; determination is deep inside of him and its exploding to get out," said the Asian man with genuine concern. Dr. Bright's eyes gleamed with approval, it was the first normal look on his face all night. Trying to figure out what was going on , Folks stuck out his hand to introduce himself. "Good to meet you, I'm Folks," he said to the Asian man.

The man just looked at him and smiled, then very slowly said, "***Yes you are***!" At the same time, a door behind Dr. Bright and the Asian man casually slid open and the two men walked inside and the door slid closed behind them. Folks was awestruck! Out of the corner of his eye, he saw a wall blink on like a T.V screen. "Breaking News tonight, three killed and twenty-two injured as what authorities say an earthquake ripped through streets and buildings at and around 5th and Market streets," the news reporter firmly stated.

Earthquake, Folks thought

"More on that story tonight at eleven," said the news reporter.

The T.V. blinked and became a wall again. "They call me Zig-Zag, and baby I heard a lot of good things 'bout you!" said a man who had been seated in the corner. He stood up and looked Folks straight in his eyes. "You going to save all this, huh?" said the man.

Zig- Zag was a dark skinned man dressed in full gang banger attire. "Don't you hear me talking to you, man?".

Folks was stunned! "Who are you?" he asked

"I'm Zig-Zag. No need to ask who you are, man, you the finest! Kings amongst kings the one and only Folks Bell" Zig-Zag stated with a devilish smile. "No need on asking about Dr. Sala, he and the connection are long gone, men like that can't stay around in this shit!" said Zig-Zag.

"Who are you?" asked Folks very slowly.

"A better question is who is Raul Testo?" stated Zig-Zag.

Folks just looked at the man for a second.

"See, Raul got all of us by the balls, that mother-fucker and his machines are going to cause a lot of chaos. You know he already got enough information from those papers that he took out of that bank to identify and possibly locate the 24 elders!" stated Zig-Zag matter of factly. "The son of Lilith has awakened and all!" said Zig-Zag.

"Wait a minute. Are you ok?" said Folks. "Who the hell are you? Where the hell is Dr. Bright? I don't know if you know this but we are scientist, and the news just announced that there was a..." Before Folks could finish talking Zig-Zag cut him off and finished the sentence. "Massive 7.2 earthquake attack in the middle of Center City, Philadelphia, some hurt, some killed, some just scared as shit. Nobody knows what the fuck is going on," said Zig-Zag. "What you think I'm here for Folks? Do you know who Raul Testo is?" asked Zig-Zag.

"You mean the guy from the stories? The mad scientist guy? The one who would make machines to destroy in the 1800s?" asked Folks curiously.

"Well it ain't no story, and the bastard is still making machines. See, when the devil hides he does it in plain sight. Raul ain't no myth and the people he is with is damn sure for real!" said Zig-Zag. Folks continued to listen while Zig-Zag spoke. "Raul is a nightmare, smarter than any one - hundred men, and as deadly as a bullet. Dr. Sala wanted me explain things to you. He felt that I could better relate certain information to you for now on end."

"Information like what ?" Folks asked sharply. "Information that's going to help you seek out and destroy Raul The Cool and his machines!" Zig-Zag sharply stated. Folks could see the man had two guns , one on each hip, this made the young astronomer very uneasy. Folks felt that if he didn't make any sudden moves and kept talking, at least to entertain the man, he would be ok for now!

Just then there was a knock on the door. Zig-Zag yelled "MOVE" and pushed Folks out of the way. Gun fire burst through the door, Zig-Zag grabbed Folks by the arm and led them over to a spiral staircase and told Folks to run upstairs. As Folks ran up the steps he turned and could see Zig-Zag pull out two guns and started shooting back at the doorway. Zig-Zag's guns sounded like cannons, as did the shots coming through the doorway! " Folks, top of the steps make a left" ordered Zig-Zag as he was now climbing the spiral staircase and shooting at the same time. When Folks reached the top of the steps he made a left and ran down the long hallway. Before Folks knew it Zig-Zag ran past him, and burst through a door at the end of the hallway. Folks could see Zig-Zag shooting as he ran past a threshold of the doorway. "Folks, upstairs," ordered Zig-Zag as he covered Folks with gun fire. Folks ran to the top of the steps and stopped, he looked backed and Zig-Zag was coming up the steps. When Zig-Zag reached the top of the steps he opened a small door to a code box and punched in five digits. The door slid opened open and Zig-Zag rushed Folks into the room. The room was filled with guns all neatly placed on the walls like artwork. Zig-Zag started grabbing ammunition while mumbling, "I thought we had more time," in a sarcastic tone of voice. After he grabbed what he needed, Zig-Zag moved over to the north east corner of the room and punched in a code on another box. This time a square door slid aside in the floor to reveal what looked like a long sliding board, and Zig-Zag pushed Folks down the chute. Zig-Zag could hear banging on the door. Before he went down the chute he placed a small hockey puck shaped device on the floor next to the chute and pushed a button and slid down the chute. A second later the entity burst into the room and the device exploded shattering the room. The sliding board led Folks and Zig-Zag to a garage like room in which there was a brand new dark blue Lamborghini Gallardo. Zig-Zag threw his bag of arms in the trunk and told Folks to get in the car. Zig-Zag started the car and burst through the garage door like a bat out of hell and sped up the block towards City Line Ave. At this time four cars were behind them in pursuit. Zig-Zag leaned his right arm out the window and shot at the cars as he drove onto the highway. One of the cars came up paralleled to the driver's side of Zig-Zags car. Zig-Zag threw an explosive which stuck on the cars windshield and it exploded the car into a fiery wreck! Another car was catching up fast, Zig-Zag threw the emergency brake on and sent the car around 180 degrees and began shooting at the approaching car all while traffic zoomed by blowing horns in sheer terror! Zig-Zag's bullets struck the driver causing him to swerve sideways blocking on coming traffic. Zig-Zag turned the Gallardo back around, and he and Folks sped down the highway.

CHAPTER 2

Raul Testo sat on a bone white leather chaise in an upstairs room in an abandoned church. A very sickly looking man dressed in a tuxedo came into the room, stood there and looked at Raul for a few seconds, then said, "You are requested to be seen, sir."

"Well that's great Jeeves, thank you," Testo sarcastically said as he stood up from the chaise.

The man was not amused, and Testo could care less. As they approached a door, the man stopped in his tracks and Testo kept walking towards the door never looking back. The door opened on its own and Testo just stood there in the threshold.

A tall, stocky man stood in the room staring out of a window. "Hello, Mr. Testo, sorry to keep you waiting."

Testo smiled. "Have the papers?" the man asked Testo.

When Testo looked in the man's eyes he saw pure evil, which he didn't mind because he and Testo were two of a kind, but Testo knew what and who he was dealing with. Testo handed the man an envelope. The man looked at the papers like an evil kid on Christmas day. He then looked at Testo with admiration. "Mr. Testo, there is another problem, a major problem! I was wondering if you could help me with it?" the man asked.

"I'd be obliged to!" said Testo. "There is a man who is extremely important, unfortunately not to me, this man is more powerful than he believes, this should be a weakness that you could prey upon! However Mr. Testo this man's heart will never stop, and I need to rid my world of this man!" said the stocky man.

"Should be no problem," said Testo.

"Oh, but there will be, you can not take this man lightly, he is an asset to his people and a steadfast warrior. I can guarantee you've never seen the likes of him," stated the man.

"Yet, I'm willing to go after him!" said Testo.

"Good man, Mr. Testo! You see, Mr. Testo, this man is important to his people, important because most believe he is the only man that can stop me. His people will stop at nothing to prepare and protect him, and since the second you took those papers that is exactly what they have been doing. Preparing him to fulfill his prophecy!"

"What's his name?" Testo asked.

"Folks Bell!" the man answered.

Folks sat in the passenger seat of the sports car in shock. "Folks! Folks! Folks, snap out of it!" Zig-Zag demanded as he shook Folks to get his attention.

Folks then looked at Zig-Zag. "Folks, listen close, you have something very important to understand in a very short time," Zig-Zag said.

"Where's Dr. Bright!" Folks blurted out.

"He's ok, Folks, he's fine. You can trust me on that, you can trust me on everything!"stated Zig-Zag.

"Well where is he?!" Folks asked sternly.

"You're a special person, Folks. Dr. Bright knows that, we all know that! That shit you seen on the news about the earthquake, it was caused by a man named Raul Testo, and his ass is dangerous as hell!"

"Dangerous how?" Folks interrupted.

"Dangerous because this a genius with a mind of a demon. He caused that quake in Center City. He makes these machines that send vibrations through a structure and back to the machine, the friction builds up and BAM! Instant earthquake," Zig-Zag stated.

"So he's a terrorist?" asked Folks.

"He's a terrorist, murder, the mutha-fucka is crazy!" said Zig-Zag as he pushed down on the accelerator. "He wasn't there for any terrorist shit," Zig-Zag said while looking from the road to Folks' eyes. "Testo was there to steal information on the 24 Elders" said Zig-Zag.

Folks looked puzzled. "The 24 Elders are the most devine human beings created. They know all , they see all, they are nothing you could ever imagine. The most wicked man to hold the world hostage is after the

Elders," said Zig-Zag. Just then, Zig-Zag stopped talking and looked over at Folks. "You don't believe me do you?" he asked.

"Well I know something is going on, that's a given. I'm just trying to wrap my head around it," Folks said.

"Well wrap your head around this. If you don't kill Testo the whole world is fucked!" stated Zig-Zag.

Moments later, Zig-Zag and Folks pulled in front of a beautiful field with well cut grass, and flowers every where. In the middle of the field was a swing set with a small beautiful girl leaning against one of the swing posts. *The girl looked sad*, Folks thought. As Zig-Zag exited the car, and Folks followed him they started towards the small girl. They were half way to the girl when Folks asked Zig-Zag, "What are you doing?"

"I'm taking you to meet someone, and this someone wants to meet you," said Zig-Zag.

"Who wants to meet me?" asked Folks.

By now, the two men were in front of the small girl. As Folks looked at the small girl he noticed how beautiful she was. "Will you push me?" the girl asked.

Folks stood there for a few seconds. "Where are your parents?" he asked.

The small girl just smiled. "I really could use your help. What is your name?" the girl asked.

"Folks," he said. "What's yours?"

"I'm Earth," the girl said. " So… you got me?" she then asked Folks.

"I got you!" said Folks with a smile. With that Folks began pushing the girl on the swing. As Folks was pushing he turned and noticed Zig-Zag on a cell phone. Zig-Zag looked calm on the phone, so for the moment Folks remained calm.

"Mr. Folks," the small girl said. "Life is like this swing, the more you push the further you get!"

Folks looked at the small girl for a long second then said, "That's a big observation for a small girl."

"Mr. Folks, no matter who tries to stop you, you must fight them. You must believe you can win at any cost, and by any means necessary. They are coming for you, and we can't hide you forever, so Folks you must believe. It's your only hope!"

Folks was stunned. "Who are you?" he asked.

"If you look over your shoulder you'll see," said the girl. As Folks turned to look over his shoulder, he saw the pure beauty of the grass and skies. The swing in which he was pushing the girl on gently came back and ran into Folks' legs. When Folks looked down the girl was gone, and all that lay on the swing were twelve white roses. Zig-Zag was now shoulder to shoulder with Folks. "What did she say?" Zig-Zag asked softly.

"She said to believe!" said Folks

Zig-Zag looked at Folks and cleared his throat. "Folks, like I was saying about Testo, he makes these machines that create earthquake like tremors, and the Elders believe he made one that can split the earth into two. The people that Testo works with want the Elders destroyed, and they figure the only way to get the Elders out into open is to cause a world catastrophe. The Elders would have to come out and expose themselves, thereby becoming a target. The Elders are very cunning, they saw to it a long time ago that a man would come forth with light and intelligence inside of him, and fight side by side with them to destroy this entity. Do you know who this man is?" said Zig-Zag.

Folks just looked at him, but did not reply. Zig-Zag looked Folks in the eye and said, "You, you're that man Folks!"

"So who's the girl?" asked Folks.

"She's a spirit, like a muse, she'll guide you and give you inspiration."

Folks was speechless, he did not know what to say. He looked at Zig-Zag and asked, "And who are you?"

I'm your guardian," said Zig-Zag.

"And who's this enemy?" asked Folks.

"This entity, you mean?" asked Zig-Zag sarcastically.

Folks noddded yes. "Only you know who this entity is, you know him in your heart. We all suspect who it might be, but we don't know for sure."

"Why me?" asked Folks while squinting his eyes at Zig-Zag.

"Why not you?" said Zig-Zag.

"Well what next?" asked Folks.

"Next we go to see Winty, he'll cleanse your spirit and put blessings on you!" stated Zig-Zag.

As they drove off, Folks noticed how bright the sun was shining. Zig-Zag kept pushing down on the accelerator with his face switching back and forth from worry to determination. " Want to know how I became your guardian?" Zig-Zag asked.

"I was wondering," Folks said with a sly smile. "A long time ago I was a different man. There was no stronger force than me. I ruled a gang of 50,000 soldiers. Many men died by my hands. At any rate I was murdered, and that's when the connection came through the light and offered me a deal."

"The connection?" Folks asked.

"Yeah, the old Asian man that Dr. Bright introduced you to back at the house. He basically said that if I help you he would see to it that I get forgiveness, and I got to tell you ,with all the lives that I ruined, that's what I want, FORGIVENESS. Forgiveness from my self," said Zig-Zag.

A little while later Folks and Zig-Zag pulled in front of a small building on South Street. "We're here," said Zig-Zag. "Ready?" he asked Folks.

"Ready." The two men got out of the car and walked to the front door of the small building. Folks noticed the wind was blowing gently.

Zig-Zag tapped on the screen door lightly, and a few seconds later a woman opened the door. She was a short, round, older woman, with her hair in tiny dredlocks. Her eyes had fire in them, and she kept making a teeth sucking sound with her mouth. When the two men entered through the door, the woman looked at Zig-Zag with a smile and said, "Wappen Zig-Zag ?" in a very strong Jamaican accent.

"Hey, Mujolie," Zig-Zag said with a smile.

"So this is he?" asked the woman while making teeth sucking sound with her mouth. " Good to meet you,"she said to Folks in her thick Jamaican accent.

"You too," said Folks.

"I'm Mujolie, me *gwan show you a ting or two about voo-doo. Me gwan show you a man, a wicked man! You be safe like that now Folks.*"

Folks was hesitant but something inside him told him to go along with it. He looked at Zig-Zag with a " are you coming" glance.

"Naw, man, this is for your eyes only, brotha," Zig-Zag said with a smile.

"Come now star," Mujile said to Folks.

As Folks walked down the hall he could smell incense and alcohol. The song "Voodoo Woman" by Nina Simone, could now be heard as Folks and Mujoile approached a door. When Mujolie opened the door, Folks could see an elderly man around eighty, sitting calmly in a chair. Next to the man was a cage with a chicken in it, on top of the cage was an assortment of candles and religious icons. Over against another wall was a cage with two black mamba snakes inside. The elderly man stood up and put his hands on each of Folks' shoulder and smiled deeply at him. Folks looked at the man and realized that he saw the man before, in an old picture that Dr. Bright showed him in which the old man and Dr. Bright were on an archeological dig in West Africa.

At that moment the man began to speak. " Oh my boy, a precious one you are. I'm Winti"! The man had an African accent, and Folks remembered Dr. Bright telling him that Winti was a very wise man in Africa. Dr.Bright told Folks that he invited Winti on the archeological dig for that reason alone.

"You're in good hands star," said Mujolie as she left the room.

Winti started to hum and went into a trance while moving in a dance like motion around Folks. Immediately Folks noticed rain beating against a window in the room. Winti reached down and grabbed the chicken out of the cage. Next he picked up a vodka bottle and took a mouthful. He then spit the vodka all over Folks and the chicken. In a swift movement Winti pulled a blade and cut the chicken's head off! He then smeared blood on Folks' shirt. By this point Folks was in shock, and he began to feel drugged. As his mind started to race Winti called to Folks to relax. "Stay focused, stay focused, boy," Winti whispered.

The rain against the window was getting heavier, and lightning was now beginning to flash. All Folks could hear was the pace of his own heart. Winti soon reached into the cage of the black mamba snakes, and picked them both up and sat them on the floor. Folks' eyes began to grow heavy. He blinked a few time and all of a sudden found himself in the desert. There was nothing around him as far as the eye could see except for two huge stone blocks that sat about 20 feet away. Folks turned around and noticed that one of the snakes slithering towards him. He could hear the hiss. As Folks turned to run two lions came rushing past him and attacked the snake destroying the black mamba. Folks started running through the desert. Another snake was headed for Folks. Before it got to him two more lions rushed the snake. Folks looked up, and saw Winti in the distant dressed in white garments. As Folks ran toward Winti he could hear a voice telling him to be calm. " Relax, boy the lions are for you. For every one enemy, you have two friends," the voice whispered. Folks stopped running and became calm. He noticed that standing behind Winti were thousands of lions standing at attention like well trained soldiers. Behind him Folks could hear a thunderous roar approaching, like lightning moving across the ground. He could see a bright glow that shook the ground violently as it got closer. Folks did as the voice said and remained calm, but inside he felt violence and chaos building. The lightning and rumbling stopped and there stood the tall stocky man breathing hard. His chest moving up and down like a mad animal. The man was blindfolded but seemed to know exactly where Folks was standing. " I cannot see you, but I smell you. I can smell your rage and fear. You are not sure of yourself, not sure at all. Hmm, this is what the Elders picked," said the man in a sinister voice. Winti looked at Folks and could see that he was in a blank stare. Winti knew that the entity was getting to Folks.

"The boy is strong! You misunderstand! What you feel is defeat," said Winti.

"Let him say it!" said the man.

Without hesitation Folks said, "What you feel is defeat!"

The man rushed toward Folks, and grabbed him by the neck. Folks' arm flew up and knocked the man's arm off of his neck. Folks then hit the man full blast in the chest. The entity flew back then jumped up and kicked Folks in the face twice. Folks blocked a third kick and came down on the entity's rib cage with a strong elbow. The entity grabbed Folks by the head and flipped him to the ground face first. The entity then jumped high in the air and came down smashing his knee into Folks' back. The entity stayed in this position for a few seconds to enjoy the moment. Then he got up and pulled Folks to his feet. Without hesitation Folks hit the entity full force in the chest, neck and face. The entity blocked a fourth punch to the face and threw a punch back at Folks. The punch connected but did not faze Folks much. " You may not be sure of yourself, but your rage is strong!" said the entity in a fighting stance.

Folks also stood in a fighting stance. The wind blew desert sand all around as the two fighters stood facing each other some thirty feet apart. Folks charged at the entity. When he got close the entity threw a punch at him. Folks blocked the punch, then the entity connected with another punch. Folks hit the entity with a punch and followed through with an elbow to the entity's neck. The entity threw both fist into Folks chest knocking him back. Folks charged, and the entity spinned around throwing Folks into one of the two stone pillars. Folks hit the stone pillar hard and slumped to the ground. Lying there looking up at the sky Folks could see the entity standing over him looking down. Before Folks knew it the entity reached down and hit him in the face hard. Folks was now bleeding. The entity kept hitting Folks in the face over and over again. Folks no longer felt the pain but instead could feel himself blacking out. The entity reached back to hit Folks one more time, and before he blacked out he saw six lions leap over his head and knock the entity off of him. Folks lay there and blacked out to the vibrations of the thunderous fight between the entity and the lions.

CHAPTER 3

A shiny black 1967 Cadillac slowly pulled on to South Street in the dead of night and parked about fifty-feet from the building that Folks and Zig-Zag went in to earlier. The back window of the Cadillac rolled down and there sat Raul Testo smoking a cigarette. After a few minutes Testo's cell phone rang to the tune of " sorrow, tears, and blood" by Fela Kuti. "Yes" Testo answered.

"On location?" the head entity asked strongly.

"The hunt is on," said Testo. He hung up and went back to watching the building. After a while Testo saw Zig-Zag come out of the building followed by Folks who although looked tired, had a new air of strength to him. As Folks and Zig-Zag pulled off Testo got out of the car and casually walked over to the building. When he got to the front door he just stood there for a second as if he was studying the door of the building. Then Testo kicked the front door in with the force of three men. As the dust and debris cleared Testo could see Mujolie running into the front room. "Blood clot, what's gwan on"! screamed Mujolie.

"What's going on is your death! You're physic, you should already know!" said Testo. Testo then shot Mujolie. As Testo turned around he could see the old man Winti standing there. Testo looked at Winti very coldly then said, "Now you and I need to talk too!"

Folks was sitting in Zig-Zag's car at a stop light when Zig-Zag's cell phone rang. "Zig-Zag," he said into the phone.

A car behind Zig-Zag's started to beep the horn. "Come on, move the car!" yelled the driver.

Folks looked at Zig-Zag and could tell by his face that something was wrong. Zig-Zag slowly pulled around the corner and parked against the curb. "Later!" Zig-Zag said into the phone and hung up. He looked at Folks and said, "Winti and Mujolie are dead. That was the connection on the phone he said Testo is after us!"

Just then a single gun shot burst out the windshield of their car. Folks and Zig-Zag ducked down as much as they could, and Zig-Zag peeled out, screeching rubber, out of the parking spot. Before they reached the corner another gunshot hit the back of the car. Zig-Zag made a sharp right and crashed about twenty feet down the street. As the smoke was clearing the two men began to crawl out of the wreck when another gunshot hit the car just above Folks' head who was now on the ground. "Get up, get up, get up!" Zig-Zag demanded to Folks in a hiss of a whisper. Zig-Zag could now see the Cadillac slowly rolling up the street. People were running everywhere. "Shit," said Zig-Zag who then pulled two 9 mm hand guns from his waist and began to shoot back at the Cadillac coming towards them. Zig-Zag and Folks started running. "Folks, stick with me!" called Zig-Zag. The two men started running down a near by alley. "Testo is sneaky ass shit, I'm going to kill that motherfucka as soon as I get the chance!"

At the end of the alley the two men stopped running and started to walk in a fast pace as to try and fit in as much as possible. They kept this pace for about a block then "BOOM!" Another gunshot. This time it grazed Folks' arm and he fell down. As he did Zig-Zag leaned down towards Folks and asked, " Are you ok?"

"Yeah, can you see him? Is he coming?"

Zig-Zag looked around, again he seen nothing coming towards them just people running away from the gun shots. Folks and Zig-Zag could hear police sirens wailing in the distance. Zig-Zag then helped Folks up and the two men started moving down the street. All of a sudden the ground started shaking violently like an earthquake. The two men knew it was no earthquake but Testo's machine. *Where was Testo?* Zig-Zag wondered , guns in hand looking round for any sight of him. Zig-Zag turned around to look for Folks, and was hit in the face by a closed fist. Zig-Zag fell back and started shooting in the direction of the blow. Testo had already moved behind Zig-Zag and now had Zig-Zag's neck gripped in his hands. Testo hit Zig-Zag in the windpipe hard and Zig-Zag dropped his weapons. "Mr. Zig-Zag I presume?" Testo asked with a smile. He then threw Zig-Zag into a parked car. A board came crashing down on Testo's back. The board connected so hard that it shattered like glass over Testo back. Testo stumbled forward and turned around. Folks leapt forward and hit Testo with a karate style combination to his chest. Testo felt the blow but shook it off. Testo quickly hit Folks in the neck while taking his feet and sweeping Folks' legs from under him. Testo pulled a butterfly knife and lunged at Folks. The young man rolled to his side and moved quickly to get up. Folks could now see the guns about four feet away lying on the ground. Folks jumped and grabbed the guns. Zig-Zag was now up and on his feet fighting with Testo. Folks aimed the guns but Zig-Zag was in the way. Folks could now hear the police sirens about two blocks away. Testo punched Zig-Zag in the face and darted down an alley into the darkness. Folks wanted to chase after him, but knew it would be better to get Zig-Zag and get out of there. As the cops got about forty feet away from them Folks and Zig-Zag started running down the street. Cop car after cop car sped down the street after the two men. About a block and a half down Folks turned into an alley and Zig-Zag followed. By now the police helicopter was in the air and closing in on them . At the end of the alley was an indoor parking garage. The two turned into the garage as the police gave chase. Zig-Zag saw a Mercedes-Benz 600 series and ran over to it. Folks followed, while keeping an eye on their backs. Zig-Zag smashed the driver's side window out. The car's alarm went off as Zig-Zag opened the door. The two men jumped into the car. Zig-Zag pulled out a small knife and jabbed it into the steering column, the cars engine started and the two men gently pulled out of the garage. "Let me guess that was Testo?" asked Folks.

"Yeah, that bitch!" growled Zig-Zag. " Hey, how did you know that karate shit?" Zig-Zag asked .

"I don't know!" Folks answered.

"What about your arm?" asked Zig-Zag.

"It's fine. The bullet just grazed me," said Folks. "As you start to believe in yourself you will notice that you can do different things. You will automatically know things, things about knowledge, things about the future," stated Zig-Zag.

"I'm trying to understand all of this," said Folks.

"It'll come," said Zig-Zag.

"Earlier you said that was the connection on the phone. Is he with Dr.Bright? Is Dr.Bright ok?" asked Folks with great concern.

"He's cool, you'll be talking to him soon!" said Zig-Zag.

"What do you mean ?" asked Folks.

"The connection needs to talk to you, besides you have training," said Zig-Zag.

"Training?" asked Folks.

Zig-Zag justed smiled.

"Damn, I thought Testo was a myth," said Folks.

"Not at all. He's a real deal killing machine, and he does not discriminate!" stated Zig-Zag.

"So I've seen," mumbled Folks.

"His earthquake machines are pissing me off, shit Testo flip that switch and it's all over," said Zig-Zag. " He made that machine for a bigger purpose, he didn't make it to just steal those papers on the Elders," said Folks.

"How do you know?" asked Zig-Zag.

"I just get that feeling. He's going to try to use his machines on a bigger scale," stated Folks.

Zig-Zag looked at him for a moment as if he was really taking in what Folks was saying. "We have to make a stop it's time to arm up," said Zig-Zag.

The Head Entity sat in a chair inside the abandoned church. Focusing on the papers that Testo had given him, he carefully eyed the pictures of 24 different men who were on the papers. The men were from all different cultures. This didn't surprise him, the head entity had already known that the Elders were the most brilliant men from 24 different locations in the world. Each of the men were of the highest spiritually and intelligently wise. It is believed that these men posses the power to bring about world peace and spiritual awareness in humans. These 24 men hand picked a man to unite with them and control the engine that will destroy the evil of the earth. These are the men and the reasons that the head entity wanted them dead! Each one of the Elders names started with the name "star" and ended with a series of dots and lines. The head entity wasn't sure what the names meant but immediately wondered if it was a message of some sort. He rubbed his eyes hard and then sat back in the chair and took a deep breath. "Excuse me, sir, someone is here to see you," said the head entity's servant. The servant was standing in the doorway looking more pale than usual. The head entity looked at the servant in disgust. "Send him in!" he growled. A second later a ten year old Puerto Rican looking boy with a mixture of fire and evil in his eyes entered the room. The boy and the head entity just stared at each other for a few seconds, then the boy spoke. "You know who I am, you know why I am here! Where are the papers?"

The head entity was furious but he knew to not let it show and at least not for now. "I have them, but there not here," he said to the boy. The boy drew his head back and sighed. He brought his head back down and looked at the head entity very hard. "Is my image fooling you?" asked the boy directly.

"Not at all! As you said, I know who and what you are, but even still I will have to get them to you later," stated the entity matter of factly.

"You have three hours, after three hours I will be back," said the boy. The head entity just nodded. The boy turned and walked out of the room. As he walked through the hallway he saw Testo walking towards him from the end of the hallway. The boy pushed past Testo and Testo looked at the boy with fury, but kept walking towards the servant who was standing in front of the head entity's office door.

"Where is he?!" demanded Testo.

"This way, Mr. Testo," said the servant.

Testo came in to the room and , asked the head entity, "Who the hell is that kid?"

"That was no kid, and who in the hell is right!" answered the head entity.

Testo gave the head entity a puzzled looked. " That was the son of Lilith not a kid more like a monstrosity! Even by my standards. He sort of wants what we want!" said the head entity.

"How so?" asked Testo.

"The Elders hold knowledge that could be very useful for him!" said the head entity.

Testo just shrugged his shoulders and dismissed his comment. " At any rate"! Testo began. " I came at the target!"

"And?!" said the head entity.

"They made it out by the skin of their teeth," Testo said.

"But they made it out ?!" stated the head entity. Testo looked at the head entity with a smirk on his face. "Mr. Testo, take a look at these names, and tell me what you think?" asked the head entity. Testo took the page with the markings and dots and looked at it for a second. He then started reading the names as " Star 6 , Star 15 , Star 12, Star."

Before Testo could finish reading the names the head entity stopped him. "Where are you getting these numbers?" it asked.

"It's Mayan numerology, each dot stands for 1, and each line stand for 5. One dot over one line equals 6, so on and so forth, " stated Testo.

The head entity looked at Testo and smiled menacingly at him. He reached for his desk and turned his computer screen towards him, and started typing keys on the pad. "Mr. Testo, read me those names again please," it said.

Testo began reading the names, "Star 6, Star 15…" when Testo finished reading all the names the head entity smiled even more. Testo looked at the computer screen and cocked his head to the side. "It's a message!" Testo said.

"It's the number of the alphabet!" stated the head entity who had never stop smiling.

Testo began, "There are 24 Elders, and 24 letters in this message! Interesting."

"Folks is the protector of man," stated the head entity. Now both of the men had a menacing smile on their faces. As Testo smiled something out the window caught his eye. When he turned and looked he stopped smiling. Testo could see about one-thousand skeletal looking men all standing in attention in the field outside of the church. " Who are they!? he asked.

The head entity kept smiling then answered, "That's the army of the sun."

"The Son of Lilith's army?" Testo asked.

"Just a few soldiers of his not the whole army. He wants these papers on the Elders. I just wanted to decipher the message first."

"Let me guess. We don't give him the papers we go to war with them right?" asked Testo.

"That's about right!" stated the head entity.

Folks and Zig-Zag pulled the stolen Mercedes into a parking spot on North 63rd Street. The two of them walked up to a house on North 65th Street. As they approached the house Zig-Zag walked right up the front door and knocked hard. The song "pumpkin belly" by Tenor Saw could be heard from outside on the front porch. "Who is it?!" a man with a strong voice yelled from inside. The sound of several dead bolts being unlocked could be heard. Finally a muscular white man, who was six foot four with a three inch beard and a bald head opened the door. "Zig-Zag! My main man, wats happen wit'cha ya?" said A- wax through a wide smile.

Zig-Zag smiled and shook the mans hand then he and Folks entered in to the house. The house was an expensive bachelor pad with red leather sofas, a flat screen T.V. "A-wax, this is Folks! I'm kinda helping him with a big problem he has," said Zig-Zag.

While Folks and A-wax shook hands, A-wax turned to Zig-Zag and said, "Big problems, huh? Well you come to the right place."

A-wax led the two men downstairs to a room and opened the door. Two huge and very angry pit bulls came running towards the front of the door and Folks froze in fear. "Hard-Core ! Meow! Sit down!" yelled A-wax. Both dogs stopped dead in their tracks, and started wagging their tails. "Ya'll want something to drink?" A-wax asked the two men.

"We're good, thanks, man," said Zig-Zag.

All three of the men sat down and A-wax looked at Folks and said to Zig-Zag, " So, Zig, what type of problems, big problems or big ass problems."

"Big ass problems, man!" Zig-Zag said

"Care to talk about it?" asked A-wax.

Zig-Zag just looked at him, and the two men started laughing. A-wax turned to look at Folks again. Folks was looking at a 250 gallon aquarium that was embedded in the wall. A-wax started to speak, " Those are African…".

Before he could finish Folks started in, "African Cichlids from Lake Victoria. Very territorial but they are also very smart and beautiful fish."

Zig-Zag was obviously impressed. "Lake Vic… Who?"

"Lake Victoria. It's in Africa," said Folks.

"Ahh shit! I got those from World Wide Aquarium," said A-wax. A-wax and Zig-Zag started to laugh. A-wax cleared his throat, and became serious. "Big ass problems, huh gents? Well let's get ya'll some big ass problem solvers!" stated A-wax. A-wax led Folks and Zig-Zag to a back room and opened the door. The room was filled with guns, ammo, Kevlar vests and hand grenades. A-wax walked over to a wall and picked a gun off of a glass shelf. "This here fellas is the HN HERSTAL FNP-9. Small, light weight, handles like a P229 only lighter weight. For sure to be a show stopper!" said A-wax.

"Nice!" said Zig-Zag.

"Nice!" repeated A-wax with a smile. A-wax walked over to a wall, and flicked a switch. The wall with guns on it turned around to reveal more guns. "Now this! This is the STEYR TMP from Austria. Compact, and will spank ass like you brought your dad a bad report card," stated A-wax.

"Yeahh, now that's nice!" said Zig-Zag .

"You like that? Well look at this," said A-wax. "This is the FN P90 sub machine gun, it's from Belgium. Not only is it beautiful, but it has a large mag capacity. It's completely ambidexterity and it's easy to use and clean," said A-wax as if he was selling a new car to the men.

Zig-Zag started in, "We'll take four of those small 9MM's."

"Anything else?" asked A-wax with a smile.

"Yeah, strong machine guns," said Folks sternly.

"Well okay," mumbled Zig-Zag.

A-wax gave them an assortment of machine guns, grenades, c-4 and ammo. Zig-Zag looked at A-wax and smiled then asked, " Hey A-wax, are you still into cars?"

"Yes sir," A-wax quickly answered.

Zig-Zag smiled big then said, "Well there's a brand-new 600 series Benz for you sitting on the corner of 63rd Street."

A-wax thought for a second then said, "I can do that!"

Raul Testo sat in his lab which looked more like a horror house. There were monkeys in cages that looked like they were pumped full of steroids. In one part of the laboratory there were animals with limbs removed, and some of the animals were even dead. God only knows how these poor creatures met their fate. Testo was dressed in a perfectly white lab coat with gloves and protective eye glasses. He sat on a stool studying the liquids inside two test tubes. One of the liquids was green, and the other was a crystal like white substance. Testo then mixed the two liquids together. He quickly put a lid on the test tube and gently shook it. He then took a hypodermic needle out of a drawer and inserted the needle through the plastic lid of the test tube. Testo then drew up 50CC 's of the liquid mixture then put the test tube in a metal holding rack. He then walked over to a 300 gallon glass tank with 100's of white rats inside. The rats were nibbling at the glass and running on top of each other. Testo opened the lid to the glass tank and quickly squirted the liquid out of the needle and into the tank. He then pushed the button on his stopwatch and stared at the glass tank. After 12 seconds, about 30% of the rats fell dead. After another 12 seconds 40 % were dead, and inside 30 seconds all of the rats in the glass tank were dead. Testo smiled a smile that would make the devil cringe a bit. He then turned around and looked across the room of his lab at two 400 gallon glass tanks .One tank was filled with the green liquid, and the other tank was filled with the crystal like white liquid.

The old woman sat on the roof of a house that looked like a bomb hit it. She sat quietly chanting while looking up at the full moon. The scarf that was around her head hid most of her face, but when the moon light hit her face it exposed a hideously grotesque image with gray skin, rotted teeth, scars and eyes that constantly drip puss. Behind the old lady coming out of the sky and landing on the roof was the Son of Lilith. As the young boy landed gently on the roof he closed his bat like wings behind him. The young boy's wings must have had a span of 6 feet. He stood there behind the old lady for a few seconds, Then walked up on her from behind. The old lady never stopped the gentle chanting or looking at the moon. "I have the information on the 24 Elders. The head entity was reluctant to give the information too me, but then he got smart!" stated the boy. As the young boy spoke the old lady never turned around, and she never stopped looking at the moon or chanting. Her chanting did however start to gradually become louder. As the old lady's chanting became louder the boy continued to speak, "The war has begun. The head entity is in his in stages and I expect him to fight the young prodigy with all his strength." The old woman continued her stare and by now her voice was fairly loud, and lightning started to appear in the dark night sky. She started to slowly raise her arms to the sky as the boy continued, " The prodigy has his guardian angel with him and has started to believe in his gift. Soon he will shine! The young boy stopped talking and looked down for a second. The old woman's chant was now almost a scream and the lightning in the sky became very intense. Her arms were fully raised to the sky, and she was now rolling her neck around in a trance like motion. The boy raised his head back up and began to speak. "The prodigy has spoken to earth!" At that the old woman's chant turned into a blood chilling scream that filled the night. The lightning in the sky thrashed about wildly. The light from it helped to further expose the buildings around them. The buildings were dilapidated for as far as the eyes could see it resembled a scene from WWII where every building was close together in rows and they were all bombed out. Down below lions stalked about the broken street growling, as if they were in some sort of maze.

Raul Testo got out of the cab at 13th and Market Streets dressed in a black suit, pink dress shirt, white tie and a red handkerchief in the top pocket of his suit jacket. He held a brief case tight and quickly moved down the subway steps which led to the underground train system. Testo walked onto the train platform sat on a bench, and put the briefcase on his lap. About 30 small holes had been drilled into one side of the briefcase inside the briefcase were two glass cylinders the size of thermoses. In between the glass cylinders was a metal spring life device like the ones on the old fire alarms. Under the device was a digital clock set for ten minutes. A young Asian woman with dredlocks and black lipstick sat on the bench next to Testo with her laptop opened. Testo looked at her then looked away. He felt his adrenaline rising, but was calm all the same. As more and more people began to feel the subway platform Testo began to smile to himself. A song by Public Enemy named "Welcome to the Terror Dome" came blasting out of the young Asian woman's laptop. With embarrassment she fumbled around with the volume control button, but as if the button was broken she could not get the volume to lower. Over the loud song Testo could hear the train approaching the platform. A few seconds later the train pulled into the platform and stopped. The platform was filled with people getting on and off the train. Testo took the briefcase and slid it under the bench that he was sitting on. He then quickly mixed into the crowd and entered the train just as the doors were closing. The train gave a jerk then pulled of into the tunnel. After two stops down the trained pulled into the next platform. The doors opened, and Testo exited the train and moved up the steps of the subway station. Once outside Testo hailed down a cab and once again road off into the blue. Leaving a silent catastrophe close behind.

CHAPTER 4

(NEWS REPORTER) "Ladies and gentlemen this has to be the worst day in Philadelphia's history. Words cannot express the heartbreak that the city is feeling right now! Fire Rescue has reported at least 200 dead from a bio-germ catastrophe. Authorities speculate terrorist activity, but did not confirm that to be true. We strongly urge to remain calm, and authorities want everyone to remain in their homes. Again people should remain calm and stay inside! Keep tuned in to your local news channel for any and further reports. There is a significant amount of rioting both from looting and panic. Haz-mat teams are out in full force as well. People this is Peyton Eli for WBUZ. I'm now going to switch you to Stacey Craven who is on 18th and J.F K Boulevard with a live witness. (NEWS REPORTER, Stacey Craven) "Thank you Peyton. Hi I'm Stacey Craven , and I'm here talking to Richard Carman and Beverly Leinhardt, who were actually one of the first people to call 911, and report what they saw. Beverly, what did you actually see?"

"My God! I came around the corner of 9th Street onto Market and people were just falling, just like that ! I mean dead in their tracks! I. . .I . . I was in shock!" stated the female witness.

"And you Mr. Carman, what did you see, sir?" asked the reporter.

"As she said we walked around the corner and bam! I never saw anything like it. I did two tours in Nam, and that's what it reminded me of. Bodies were everywhere! I took Beverly's hand and we started running. I haven't ran that fast in twenty years!" stated the male witness.

Just then an angry person in the crowed yelled out, "It was terrorists,

I know it! The media can't try and cover this one up, everybody better get ready to fight!"

The police started making everyone move onto the sidewalk and away from the report. People were still yelling and cursing when Zig-Zag turned off the T.V. He and Folks were held up in a motel in Media, Pennsylvania. The two were waiting for a call from the connection to tell them when it was safe to come to his location. Folks was looking out the window through a slit in the shade. He had been doing this since they got there. On the bed and on the floor of the room were all the guns that A-Wax had given them. All the guns were polished and fully loaded. Folks turned to Zig-Zag and asked, "What do you think Testo gets out of this? I mean just killing people for no reason at all!"

Zig-Zag just shook his head slowly and said, "I don't know."

"He's fighting with us! So why kill innocent people?" questioned Folks.

"Yep," Was Zig-Zag's only reply as he kept standing guard by the front door. After a few minutes of silence Zig-Zag's phone rang. He answered. "All is clear," stated a man on the other end of the phone. Then the voice on the phone continued, "The location is 5457 Kingsessing Ave. There will be a laptop in the basement. All further information will be in the laptop."

"Zig-Zag, move fast and get rid of this phone faster!" Zig-Zag hung up the phone and started throwing the guns in a large duffel bag.

Folks looked at him and asked, "Time to roll?"

"Time to roll," answered Zig-Zag. Folks took one last look out of the window, and threw the strap of one of the duffel bags over his shoulder. Zig-Zag did the same. Folks then quietly took the lock off of the door and slowly peeked his head outside. Once he saw that all was clear he and Zig-Zag moved out the room and down the hallway. The two men casually walked down the steps to the main lobby, and out of the door. Zig -Zag tossed the phone in a sewage hole and the two men walked across the street to a trolley stop. After a few minutes the trolley came and the two men got on board. The trolley rolled through the suburbs headed towards Philadelphia. The people on board were all having conversations with each other about the breaking news of the day. As the trolley moved along Folks wondered about Dr. Bright. He wondered if Dr. Bright ever showed any signs that this day would come. From the window of the trolley Folks saw small children playing, and admired the fact that they didn't have a care in the world. The trolley pulled into the terminal at 69th and Market Streets and the two men got off. Zig-Zag noticed that there were more police in the terminal than usual. No doubt because of today's events the two men kept calm and walked out of the terminal without incident.

"Alright man, this is it! Now I know your nervous 'bout meeting the connection and the training and all, but you will be fine. Keep your chin up and keep swinging!" Zig-Zag said to Folks as they walked.

"What am I going to learn in training?" asked Folks.

Zig-Zag paused for a second then said, "I couldn't tell you."

Folks and Zig-Zag reached the corner of 53rd Street and Kingsessing Ave. Four men were sitting at a red light in a brand new, red Dodge Charger with chrome wheels. As Folks and Zig-Zag walked in front of their car the four men stared at them very hard. This was gang and drug territory and the two men were very out of place. The light turned green and the car slowly pulled off. A song by Ghost Face Killa named "shakey dogs" could be heard blasting from the Charger as it slowly rolled down the street. Folks started reading the address numbers and saw that they were at 5429 and he figured the house that they were looking for was just a few doors down. They reached the house. It was the last one at the end of the small row homes. The house was totally dilapidated with the windows broken out and part of the roof caved in. Folks entered the house first and he and Zig-Zag started to look for the basement door. Rats could be heard running along the baseboard of the wall. The stench of the water from the broken pipes made the smell of the house less than desirable. They spotted the door to the basement near the kitchen. Zig-Zag went to grab the doorknob, and the old wooden door fell off the hinges. Zig-Zag let go of the doorknob, and the door went falling down the basement steps. The two men then walked down the rickety steps and saw the laptop on an old wooden table in the center of the basement. Zig-Zag opened the laptop and at the top of the screen was a bomb icon that was slowly ticking and dropping at the same time. At the bottom of the screen was an icon of a man jogging in place that had the words, "follow me" under it. Zig-Zag moved the cursor to the jogging man and clicked it. The screen became black for a second then the voice of the Asian man started to speak. The connection said that a car is waiting outside with a driver and that the two men should get in. By now the icon of the bomb was getting closer to the bottom of the screen. Folks and Zig-Zag took the connections advice and quickly started up the steps and out the door to the a waiting car which then took off. The car reached the end of the block when the house that Folks and Zig-Zag just left exploded!

Testo sat in a chair in his laboratory blasting the song, "When the Levy Breaks," by Led Zeppelin. He sat there in a trance like mode while the song played on. In his hands was an old picture of a beautiful woman and a small pretty girl. As he sat in the chair he began to tremble and shake. His jaw became very tight and the picture of the woman and girl fell out of his hand right before he began to clench his fist. His tremble had long ago turned into a violent shake, and his jaw was now compressed enough to crush diamonds. Suddenly Testo jumped out of the chair and turned over a small table laden with tubes and microscopes. He then turned around and hit the center of another table with his hand breaking it to bits. Testo thrashed around violently ripping down shelves and breaking glass. Both of his hands were now bleeding to which he paid no attention. He just kept thrashing around and destroying his laboratory. Within minutes the lab looked liked a train drove through it! Testo fell to his knees gasping like a wild animal! His heart was racing as if it was going to jump out of his chest. Testo slowly began to calm himself. He put his hands over his face and left smeared all over it from his bleeding hands. He drew his hands away from his face and looked at them for a few seconds before he collapsed to the floor and passed out.

The car arrived at a large home in Willow Grove, Pennsylvania. Folks and Zig-Zag sat in the back seat for a second. When Folks looked into the rear view mirror the driver motioning with his eyes for them to exit the car. Folks calmly got out of the car and Zig-Zag followed. An old Asian man was standing next to a small bird fountain. He began to smile as Folks and Zig-Zag approached him. Folks noticed the man was rotating four apple size glass balls in his hand. "Zig-Zag," said the old man quietly while smiling. Zig-Zag and the old man looked at Folks, and studied him for a moment. "Folks, I am sorry for the way we met last time, but I have been keeping a close eye on you," said the old man calmly but very serious. Folks smiled weakly and looked down at the ground. He noticed the old man never stopped rotating the glass balls in his hand. Folks then looked up at the old man. "Folks, I am the Connection. It is a great blessing to meet you! Many men are giving their lives for you to be here, and they should," stated the old man.

Folks listened to the old man as he spoke. "Do not worry, Folks, you are as stronger than you think," said the old man. Folks looked back down at the ground, and his face went into shock. Folks was now rotating the glass balls in his hand, and didn't even realize it! Folks started to smile as he rotated the glass balls in his hand. "You are more powerful than you know," the old man said to Folks. The Connection took the glass balls from Folks' hand, then turned around and walked towards the front door. Folks and Zig-Zag followed the Connection into the house. All of the furniture was white, and everything was spotless. The floors were polished to a high gloss. Beautiful crystal vases held colorful flowers. the Connection poured Folks a glass of water. Zig-Zag walked away to look at the flowers and vases. Folks took a drink of water, and sat the glass down on a silver tray. "I have much to show you, Folks, but first I want you to see something very important," said the Connection. The Connection led Folks to a door and opened it. There was a metal staircase which led to what looked like a gymnasium. The walls were covered with what looked like ancient Egyptian hieroglyphs. "This room is for warriors," stated the Connection. Inside of the room were all types of martial arts weapons and training posts. Folks looked at the Connection. The Connection then threw his hand out at Folks' face to which Folks ducked. The Connection threw another punch, and Folks ducked that also. The Connection stood there for a second then looked Folks in the eye and smiled deeply. The Connection then drew back into a martial arts stance and yelled "YAA!" Before Folks could think he was blocking a kick from the connection. Folks ducked as the Connection spun around with a kick. The Connection then threw three full blast punches at Folks' chest. The last one connected and knocked Folks off of his balance. Before Folks got his balance, the Connection was throwing a combination of punches at him. Folks blocked a few punches, then got hit with a punch, but never flinched. Folks then jumped back, and took a defensive stance.

"YAA," Folks yelled out. At that Folks attacked the old man with a variety of combinations. The Connection grabbed Folks' fist, and flipped Folks into the air. Folks rolled to the ground, jumped up and again took his stance. "Very good, prodigy," said the Connection to Folks. Folks kept his stance. The Connection was also in his stance. The two men stood staring into each other's eyes for a few seconds. Then the Connection drew out several darts with small green features on the end of each one, and quickly threw them at Folks. Folks jumped up, and the darts hit a wooden training post. The Connection then pulled out a pair of nunchucks and started twirling them around. He began to twirl them faster and faster then lunged at Folks. Folks ducked, and moved fast so not to get hit with the nun-chucks. Folks then turned, and ran towards a wall. The Connection gave chase. Folks ran up the wall, and back flipped off of it. Now Folks was behind the Connection. The Connection spun around, and blew a handful of dust into Folks' eyes. Folks reached for his eyes, and felt a full blast kick to his chest!

"You didn't see that coming did you, prodigy?" asked the Connection. Folks, lying with his back on the ground jumped up into the tiger style karate stance. The Connection lunged at Folks. Folks ducked, and spun around at the same time with his leg extended knocking the old man off of his feet. Folks then jumped up in the air, and attempted to come down on the Connection's head. The Connection grabbed Folks' foot in mid air, and tossed him across the room.

"Damn you're good," Folks said while getting up off of the floor.

"You're not bad yourself for someone who didn't know he could do this last week!" said the Connection. Folks started running towards another wall. When he reached the wall he ran up to the ceiling, and then across. Folks jumped down from the ceiling, and landed in front of the Connection then hit him in the chest. The Connection paid the blow no attention, and jumped into the air to kick folks. Folks ducked the kick, and quickly blew a handful of dust into the old man's eyes. The Connection went down on one knee rubbing his eyes. "Didn't see that coming did you?" asked Folks now poised in his karate stance. The Connection smiled while rubbing his eyes. The Connection then tosses a smoke ball to the floor. Smoke was everywhere. "What to do now, prodigy?" asked the Connection who was now hiding in the smoke. Folks kept his defensive stance. Suddenly a force hit Folks in the chest. He stumbled back, but did not fall. Another blow hit Folks in his face. He struck back, and hit the Connection with an intense blow. The smoke started to clear, and Folks could see the Connection on the ceiling smiling at him.

As Folks wondered why the old man was smiling he looked down at himself, and saw that he was glowing a bright green color. "You are in the zone, young prodigy," said the Connection. Folks just stood there in amazement. "Finish!" demanded the Connection. Folks ran up the wall to the ceiling, and towards the Connection.

Folks threw a combination of punches striking the Connection a few times. The Connection stumbled back and returned a combination of punches of his own. None of the blows connected with Folks. Both men dropped from the ceiling to the floor. Folks stood there with his arms extended looking at himself glow green. Just then a pair of doors to the room burst open. About ten men rushed into the room, and charged at Folks. Folks struck the first man in his face with an open palm. Folks kicked the next man in his neck, dropping him to the floor. Two other men rushed at Folks, within seconds they were on the floor. The men were no match for Folks. He was dropping them in seconds!

"HALT!" yelled the Connection. The fighting stopped! The men on the floor quietly got up, and bowed to Folks and the Connection then walked out of the room. Folks glow started to fade. The Connection walked over to Folks. "Very, very good, young prodigy. When you are focused, and your mind, body, and soul are aligned you will start to glow! It is the glow that give you invincibility . You will learn to control this in time!" said the Connection.

"It felt strong, powerful!" said Folks.

"It is strong, and very powerful, but more importantly it is controllable! You must control it, prodigy!" said the Connection. The Connection led Folks to an upstairs room. Inside of the room was a large hot tub. Towels laid on a metal rack against the wall. "Take some time for yourself and relax young prodigy, come see me. There is more for you to see!" the Connection said.

"Nice work, Testo!" the Head Entity said in a pissed off voice. Testo smiled wickedly. The Head Entity squinted and scowled at Testo for a few seconds. "Testo, we are in the middle of the ultimate war, and you pull a stunt like that! Do not forget you rank and position, Mr. Testo!" said the Head Entity with disgust. Testo still held that wicked smile on his face. The Head Entity began to yell, "YOU PUT...!"

Before he could finish Testo Cut him off, "I'm sorry, did you have a loved one in that subway?" asked Testo.

"Fuck those people! You put us in the light, and there for sure to kill us!" the Head Entity screamed.

"How so?" Testo asked calmly.

The Head Entity took a deep breath and exhaled then spoke. "Folks is strong - very strong. They are training him as we speak. You don't think this wont make him come at us stronger?"

Testo's eyes burned like fire! "Do you know what plans the Son of Lilith has for you?" asked Testo, still smiling.

The Head Entity stared at Testo. "I'll tell you," Testo began. "After you provide him, and his hag of a mother with a confirmed location on the Elders, they're going to kill you!"

"Who do think you're talking to?" the Head Entity hissed.

"You know, I never heard of that little muthafuker until he came here that day. So I asked around, and I found out some very interesting things about him!" said Testo.

"Did you!?" asked The Head Entity.

Testo continued. "You see, I did the subway job for my own pleasure, fuck yours! You're half right. We're in the ultimate war, but YOU can't win! You're not made to! I want those motherfuckas to come after me. I'm made to weather the storm!"

"Are you crazy? Do you know what I can do to you, Mr. Testo?" asked The Head Entity.

"Not a goddamn thing!" answered Testo.

The Head Entity bristled at Testo. "What if, now this is just a question, but what if there were more information and papers on the Elders? Information, and papers that I didn't give to you!" Testo asked. The Head Entity snapped, and rushed towards Testo. Just then, an arrow came darting through the window, and nailed one of The Head Entity's arms to a wall. Before The Head Entity could figure out what had just happened, another arrow nailed his other arm to the wall. The Head Entity looked around wildly for the person who did this to him. Outside of the window he could see an army of skeletal looking men. The Son of Lilith knocked on the door twice before he kicked it in. When the Head Entity looked over at the door he saw the boy with a beating heart in his hand, and the butler laid dead in a pool of blood. The Head Entity looked over at Testo. Testo, still cool, put his black Fedora hat on , and flashed his wicked smile at the Head Entity. "Be cool, pussy!" Testo said before leaving out of the room.

Zig-Zag sat in a warehouse filled with all types of technology, tools and computers. Zig-Zag sat there looking at a motorcycle with no wheels. The bike just hovered in the air. A tall, nerdy, skinny kid in his twenties named "Snipps" came walking up behind Zig-Zag. "It's a Fire Bullet," said Snips.

"A Fire Bullet?" Zig-Zag said curiously.

"Shit yeah!" said Snipps.

"Whats it do?" asked Zig-Zag.

"It has dual machine gun, dual rpgs, and it's super light weight," stated Snipps.

"Is it fast?" asked Zig-Zag.

"Is it fast? It only does like 0-250 in like a second!" answered Snipps sarcastically. "So Zig-Zag, what's up with the "guy," what's he like?" asked Snipps.

Zig-Zag just looked at the nerdy kid.

"Is he cool? Can he really do all the shit they say he can do?" Snipps asked, without taking a breath.

"You sniffing computer spray or something?" asked Zig-Zag with a smile.

"Come on, Zig-Zag, tell me something about him!" pleaded Snipps.

"Do I get one of these "Rocket Bikes?" Zig-Zag asked.

"Fire Bullets!" Snipps corrected. "Where did he come from?" Snipps continued.

"Alright, alright,alright! I'll you one thing!" said Zig-Zag.

"Cool!" Snipps said.

Zig-Zag leaned in close to Snipps and said, "I noticed something about this guy that no one else noticed about him!"

Snipps' eyes widened. Zig-Zag continued. "This motherfucka has two legs!" said Zig-Zag, with a serious look on his face.

Snipps was shocked. He jerked back out of the trance Zig-Zag had pulled him into. "Zig-Zag you asshole!" Snipps said. Zig-Zag laughed, and walked away from Snipps and the "Fire Bullet."

"Whoa, what the fuck do we have here?" asked Zig-Zag.

"Oh, now you on my shit!" said Snipps.

Zig-Zag gave Snipps a sharp look.

"O.K., relax! Just joshing. It's my own creation, its called a "Black Jack 5400" Snipps said proudly. Zig-Zag was very interested. The creation that Snipps spoke of was basically a hand held cannon. A black gun about the size of a compact 9mm, with an extended clip. "Zig-Zag, the Black Jack is lightweight, holds thirty-five in the mag., one in the chamber it fires twice as fast as any Uzi or Mack 10, 11,12, or whatever the fuck! And, and it hits harder than an AK47!" said Snipps.

Zig-Zag was in love! "Look here, revenge of the nerds!" he joked.

"Fuck you," snapped Snipps.

Zig-Zag smiled. "I'm gonna need two Black Jacks, and two Speeder Bikes," said Zig-Zag.

"FIRE BIKES!" screamed Snipps.

"Fire Bikes!?" asked Zig-Zag.

"Damn you, I meant Fire Bullets, yeah Fire Bullets!" said Snipps. Both of the me started to laugh. Zig-Zag then began to play box with Snipps. Zig-Zag dodged a couple of Snipps weak attempts at punching. The two men then shook hands. "Thanks, Snipps," said Zig-Zag.

"Anytime, my man, anytime!" said Snipps.

Zig-Zag walked towards the exit the turned around to Snipps and said, "I'll tell you this. I do believe we're in good hands!"

Snipps' look was humble as Zig-Zag walked out the door.

CHAPTER 5

In the hot tub Folks fell into a deep trance. He envisioned an old man pointing him into the direction of a beautiful field of flowers. The flowers were all different colors. The wind was blowing gently across Folks' face as he stood looking at the flowers. Folks could hear the sound of the flowers as they gently blew in the wind. "This is what you have to fear, prodigy!" the old man said to Folks.

"There is nothing to fear here!" said Folks.

"Then there is nothing to fear, is there, prodigy?" asked the old man. "Fear is here!" said the old man pointing to his head. "But fear is not here!" said the old man. This time pointing towards the field of flowers. "Believe in yourself," the old man whispered. Folks went walking towards the field of flowers. He could see the little girl named earth on a swing, just like he had before.

"Earth, is that you?" asked Folks.

"I'm going to swing really high," Earth said to Folks.

"Good for you," Folks said.

"What's your name again?" Earth asked.

As Folks said his name, Earth said it with him. "Folks, yes that's right. They talk about you! Did you know that?" said Earth.

"They who?"

"Them! The flowers, the trees, the winds. They that you know spirits, that your soul is righteous enough to understand!" Earth said.

"Understand what?" asked Folks.

"That the destruction is coming! That if you don't stop Testo, he will destroy me!" Earth said slowly.

"Why would he want to destroy you?" Folks asked.

"He hates pretty! He hates goodness! Testo suffered a great tragedy some time ago. He has not forgot, and he will never forgive! He is engrossed in hate!" said Earth.

"Why?" asked Folks

Earth looked at Folks with her big brown eyes, and said, "In a tragic accident Testo lost his wife and daughter. It was about one-hundred years ago. Testo was working with highly volatile chemicals when his house exploded. The chemical mixture killed his wife and daughter, but made him almost immortal," said Earth in a sweet child-like voice.

"How so?" Folks asked.

"Nobody knows what chemicals Testo used, but whatever they were the had a bad reaction to him. Testo was locked in prison by the authorities after the accident. The chemicals made him go mad in the prison. His cell walls were covered in scratch marks as if he was trying to claw his way out. One day after months of no noise coming from his cell an explosion happened! It killed one-hundred and thirty -four people. When his cell was checked, Testo was gone! This was in 1897, and he has been terrorizing the world ever since!"

It started to rain lightly, and a rainbow appeared in the sky. Folks and Earth stood there looking up at the sky admiring its beauty. "I love that!" said Earth.

Folks smiled. A comet shot across the sky with its multicolored tail flaring like a small sun. When Folks looked down, Earth was gone. When Folks came out of the trance, he laid in the tub feeling relaxed. There was a towel on a metal rack next to the large tub. Folks then saw his clothes neatly folded on a small bench. He got dressed and left the room. Outside was a large lobby, and seated at the far end of the lobby was the Connection. The Connection got up and walked towards Folks and asked, "Earth is a smart girl isn't she?"

Folks smiled and said, "Yes she is."

"Did she tell you about Testo?" asked the Connection.

"Yes!" Folks said.

"He is a very dangerous man, Folks! Your life will be greatly jeopardized if you go up against this man! There is a great chance that you could die!" stated The Connection.

"But if I am chosen, if this is my calling…I accept," said Folks.

The Connection smiled, and said, "They knew you would say that!"

"They? Who?" Folks asked.

The Connection looked past Folks. As he did Folks caught his eye, and turned around. Standing on the other side of the lobby were twenty - four men, all of different nationalities. Folks just looked at the men for a second. Within that second Folks had mentally recorded all of the mens' faces. One of the twenty-four men stepped forward towards Folks. He could feel that he was in the presence of men with supreme wisdom. The Elder walked right up to Folks and spoke. "Folks, we thank you for helping us! You grew to become every bit of the person that we thought you would be."

Folks just listened to the Elder as he spoke. Suddenly, the Elder stopped talking, but Folks could still hear him.

"This must have all been very trying for you Folks," said the Elder. Folks paid no attention to the comment. Instead he was focused on the fact that he heard the Elder's voice in his head.

"How did you do that?" asked Folks.

"I didn't, you did," said the Elder.

"How?" asked Folks with a confused look on his face.

The Elder just smiled at Folks. Another Elder came walking up to Folks. "Hello, prodigy, I am Star 6, and I couldn't be more pleased to stand in front of you!" said the 2nd Elder.

"That goes for all of us," said the 1st Elder. "Folks, as you know there are forces that want to destroy us, and the earth. We knew that this was coming for a long time, and for a long time we searched for the right person to head this fight, which we refer to as The Ultimate War! We did not find him! We almost gave up hope, until we met you!" said Elder Star 6. Folks stood there listening to the Elder. "Come Folks, the others want to meet you." said The Elder.

Folks was greeted by the rest of the Elders. When the greetings were finished, Elder Star 20 looked at Folks and asked, "What is a righteous man who does not know that he is righteous?"

Folks thought for a second then answered, "An unrighteous man." All twenty-four Elders smiled.

CHAPTER 6

Dr. Sala C. Bright sat in a house on the mainline when his cell phone rang. "Speak!" said Dr. Bright.

"Ahh the infamous Dr. Bright," Testo said with a deadly hiss.

Dr. Bright was shocked, no one was supposed to have this number except for one top ranking agent. "Don't even wonder if I'm going to kill Folks or not, he won't be joining this war!" said Testo.

Dr. Bright was furious, but could only manage to swallow his own saliva.

"Yeah you feel me," said Testo into the phone.

"I would think that The HEAD entity would make his own phone calls," Dr. Bright said sarcastically.

"He probably would, if it wasn't for two very good reasons. First., This isn't his call, and second he is dead!" stated Testo.

"Good for him," said Dr. Bright.

"Dr. Bright, let me ask you something," said Testo.

"I'm listening," said Dr. Bright.

"What's so special about Folks?"

"He's not you!" said Dr. Bright through a closed jaw.

Testo laughed, and then sighed. "This world owes me something Dr .Bright! I was never prey! I had thoughts and theories that wouldn't come around until the next century!" said Testo , while raising his voice.

"I could care less about your mind, Testo!" said Dr. Bright sternly.

"Well maybe you'll care about the plans that I have!" said Testo. Dr. bright didn't respond. "I'm going to continue my public attacks, I'm going to kill that fucker, Folks, and his friend, Zig-Zag, then I'm going to split the world in two," said Testo.

"You're the devil!" hissed Dr .Bright.

"The devil!?" said Testo. "No, Dr. Bright, I'm a whole nother thing, good day!

Dr. Bright hung up the phone. He knew he had to leave the location for it was not safe to be there anymore. He quickly grabbed a high powered hand gun from a small weapons stash. As Dr .Bright walked past a window he stopped in his tracks at what he saw outside. Testo stood in front of a 1974 all black Cadillac with a sinister look on his face. Before Dr. Bright could move the house exploded violently.

Zig-Zag was showing Folks the "Fire Bullet" motohover bike when The Connection came into the garage at the location. "Zig-Zag, I need to talk to you!" demanded The Connection with a serious look on his face.

"Okay," Zig-Zag said. "Folks keep checking these bike out, there super cool!"

"Cool!" Folks said, but at the same time looking at The Connection. Folks knew that something was wrong! He waited until Zig-Zag and The Connection left the room then he followed them. Folks watched the two men, as they walked down the hallway. At the end of the hallway was a room. The Connection punched a code into a panel that was next to the door. The door to the room slid open, and then slid closed after the two men entered. Folks ran down the hallway, and punched a code into the panel box. The door opened. Folks was a little surprised that he knew the code, but at the same time knowing the code felt natural to him. He quickly put that thought on hold. Folks was more concerned about what The Connection didn't want him to know. Folks felt that what The Connection had to say to Zig-Zag would be epic, but horrible at the same time. Folks quickly moved through the doorway, and up the steps in front of him. At the top of the steps Folks could see a door at the end of a hallway just closing. Folks slowly moved down the hallway, and listened with his ear against the door. Folks was extremely quiet as he listened at the door. It surprised him more when he felt himself slow his heartbeat down so to not give a vibration off at the door. Folks was very interested in what was going to be said to Zig-Zag in that room. He slowly turned the knob to the large metal door, and peeked inside. In a short distance he could see

The Connection, Zig-Zag, and a very beautiful women with red hair and green eyes. The woman had a sad, and worried look on her face, but she also stood strong like a soldier. "What's up Valhalla?" Zig-Zag said to the women.

"Nothing, Zig-Zag," said the woman in a soft voice.

Zig-Zag looked at The Connection, and without hesitation asked, "What's wrong?"

Valhalla looked at Zig-Zag with a tear in her beautiful green eye, and softly said, "Dr. Bright is dead!"

Zig-Zag's face went pale and full of shock.. Zig-Zag looked down at the floor, and with a soft voice asked, "How, Valhalla?"

Valhalla took a deep breath then said, "Testo blew up the location where Dr .Bright was. Seems that Testo called Dr. Bright on a secured cell line. We're down loading the conversation now! Seconds after that his location exploded.

"Wait a minute! How'd Testo get Dr .Bright's secured cell number? More importantly, how'd he get his location?" asked Zig-Zag. The Connection gave a slow head shake. "It's gotta be a snitch!" said Zig-Zag.

"Not even, I locked his cell phone myself, and I was also in charge of his location," said Valhalla.

Zig-Zag shook his head. Folks felt like vomiting! Dr. Bright was his world, he taught Folks everything. Folks turned and moved back down the hallway to the staircase. He turned and looked back at the door that The Connection was in then walked down the steps and through the first metal door.

CHAPTER 7

Lilith sat perched on top of a roof. In the distance she could see her son's army approaching fast. In the air she could see her son's wings stretched out like a bat. The army stopped just short of the house that Lilith sat atop. Lilith's son gently landed on the roof. "Come here, son. Let me take a look at you," said Lilith in her hag like voice. The Son of Lilith retracted his bat like wings, and walked over to his mother.

The boy's face shined like a bright star in the moonlight. Lilith reached her skeleton like hand out, and gently caressed the boy's face. "Dr. Bright is deceased!" said the boy.

"Even good men's days are numbered in these times," said Lilith.

"The Head Entity tried to keep some information from us! He will not be a problem for us again!" said the boy. Lilith smiled at this news. Her teeth were yellow and black like corn that was left to dry in the sun. Her smile faded as she began to speak. "Who is this Testo? What is his purpose?"

The boy shook his head lightly then said, " I'm not sure. His heart is dead set against Folks and the Elders."

A curious look came over Lilith's grotesque face. "What purpose I wonder. A tragedy, and a feeling of betrayal no doubt! But what!" the hag said.

"Would you like me to find out?" asked the boy.

Lilith just shrugged her shoulders and said, "No worries, it will all come out in time."

"Have you the papers on the Elders yet?" she then asked the boy.

"I believe so. Only thing is there vague. There is no indication of a location," said the boy.

"Huh! This is cat and mouse game at it's finest!" hissed Lilith. The old lady then looked away from her son's face, and up at the sky that was filled with stars. "Out of a beautiful day, comes a horrible night! Testo seems like the calm before the storm!" Lilith said.

"He is just a man. He can die like the rest!" said the boy.

Lilith smiled at the boy .She cleared her throat then said, "This will be interesting! Watching this play out."

The boy smiled devilishly. He then walked to the edge of the roof and shouted, "NIM NIM!" All of the skeleton soldiers down below stood at attention and shouted back, "NIM NIM!" The boy's wings sprouted out just as he leapt off the edge of the roof. His soldiers followed on foot. Lilith just watched as the boy moved of into the night's sky.

The Connection came walking out of the room that Folks was in when Zig-Zag and Valhalla approached him. "How's he doing?" Zig-Zag asked.

"He's doing!" said The Connection.

"Poor guy! He goes to sleep one night and wakes up to this shit," said Valhalla.

"Did you put someone on Testo?" The Connection asked.

"I have five top men on him as we speak!" said Valhalla.

"Yeah, and soon as they get a location his ass is done!" said Zig-Zag.

One of the guards came running down a spiral staircase, and went up to The Connection. "Sir, you have to come quick, Testo's on the line and he's asking for you!" said the guard.

"Valhalla, you check the grounds area. I'll do a bomb sweep!" said Zig-Zag.

The Connection and the guard hurried off .

When they reached the room , another guard waved The Connection over to a seat, and handed him an ear piece. "Line one, Sir. Try and keep him talking were working on getting a trace," said the guard.

The Connection nodded and cleared his throat. "I suppose that I'm the man you needed to speak to," said The Connection.

"You're one of them," said Testo.

"Well here I am, Mr. Testo, let's talk," The Connection said calmly.

"Many things have brought us together, but to me passion is at the top of that list! I hold passion very dear! It's one of those things that can make you or destroy you. As I have destroyed some of your passion when I killed Dr. Bright!" said Testo.

The Connection looked at one of the guards as he felt himself growing angry. "How can I help with your passion Mr. Testo?" asked The Connection calmly.

Testo sighed then began, "A long time ago when I was a different person I took passion for granted. I mattered to a couple of people, and I took that for granted. These days, I'm a changed man! I had my eye on your organization for a long time. Your Elders are perfect, which personally makes me fucking sick! Yet and still the world could care less about them. People murder, they rob each other, babies are born addicted to drugs. People on the whole could give a shit! I'm giving the "whole" a wake up call! You can thank me later."

"I agree with you, Mr. Testo, the world can be a cold and dangerous place, but not all are bad. What I don't agree with is innocent people being killed. How does that bring about justice ?" The Connection asked.

Valhalla came into the room and whispered, "Grounds clear, and being monitored, Sir!"

The Connection shook his head in approval. "Justice! Shit don't talk to me about justice! I'm going to destroy The Elders, and this world! I'm going to give it all the pain it has given me!" said Testo.

Just then Zig-Zag came into the room, and reported that there were no bombs on the ground.

The Connection put the conversation on speaker. "So, speaking of who I'm going to kill, where's Folks?"

The room went quiet as Folks walked in. "You killed the best person in my life Testo! You wanted my attention, you got it!" said Folks.

"Shark has fangs," Testo said then hung up the phone.

"Damn! We couldn't get a trace!" said a guard.

Zig-Zag moved closer to Folks and asked, "How you holding, man?"

"I'm o.k.," said Folks, not believing his own words.

"Hang in there," said Zig-Zag.

"Good to meet you, I'm Valhalla."

Folks looked at the woman, and noticed her beautiful green eyes. "Good to meet you too, I'm Folks."

"I know!" said Valhalla with a smile. "I'm sorry about Dr. Bright." said Valhalla.

"Thank you," Folks said gently.

The Connection came over to Folks and said, "We didn't get an exact location on Testo, but we did get a general area."

"Where!" asked Valhalla.

The Connection took a deep breath, then said, "Near the airport."

"Shit! We have to get there!" said Zig-Zag.

Folks, Zig-Zag, and Valhalla quickly moved out of the room, and down the stairs to a garage. Zig-Zag went over to one of the "Fire Bullets," and pulled a cover off of it.

"What's this?" asked Valhalla.

"It's a Fire Bullet. Dual guns, dual RPG's, and very fast!" said Zig-Zag.

"Wow! A Thunder Speedy," joked Valhalla.

"Fire Bullet!" Zig-Zag corrected.

Zig-Zag pulled the cover off of the second bike. Zig-Zag got on one of the hover bikes. Folks and Valhalla got on the other bike, with Valhalla driving. The door to the garage opened up, and the trio rode off.

Testo sat with a nervous look on his face. He felt something was wrong ever since he awoke this morning, but his pride had pushed that feeling out of his mind. Testo looked over at the baggage claim and could see police with dogs sniffing the luggage. *Fucking dogs,* he thought . Testo rubbed his palms on pants legs in an attempt to wipe the sweat off of his hands. He knew that the airport would be on high security with the past months events. Testo couldn't chance getting caught, but it was to late for him to turn back. The airport was crawling with cops. It seemed that dogs were sniffing every piece of luggage. He needed to stash the briefcase somewhere inside of the airport. The bomb had a little over ten minutes on its clock. Just then Testo got lucky. A commotion about fifty feet away from him caused the police near him to leave and investigate what was going on. Testo sprung off of the bench he sat on, and walked over to a bar that was about ten feet away. He ordered a drink and sat the briefcase on the floor. The bartender came back with his drink, and Testo took a sip then moved the case under the stool next to him by giving it a shove with his foot. This moved the briefcase out of eye sight. He then left a twenty dollar bill on the counter, and walked out of the door. He passed a through a lobby and got on an escalator. As he got close to the bottom Test could see five cops.

One officer was on the radio, and the other four looked up at him as if they were getting some information on him. Testo put his hand under his jacket, and on his gun. Suddenly cops swarmed the top of the escalator. "Excuse me! Sir!" said one of the officers at the top of the escalator. Testo turned around, drew his gun, and started shooting.

As the cops at the bottom off the escalator drew their guns, one of them yelled, "HOLD FIRE, HOLD FIRE!" Testo jumped off the side of the escalator. Several cops at the top of the escalator started shooting at Testo. One of the cops hit Testo in his left shoulder. Testo turned, fired his gun, and hit two more officers. "He's headed towards the entrance!" one of the cops said into the radio.

Valhalla came running across the lobby to the bar. The bartender was telling someone that the man shooting just left the bar. Valhalla stopped in her tracks, turned and entered the bar. She saw the briefcase, and knew it was the bomb. Valhalla opened the case and saw the clock at a little over five minutes. She quickly detached a yellow and orange wire, and spliced them together. The bomb stopped when she did this. Valhalla sighed then she grabbed the nearest cop, and pointed out the case to him. The cop went to check out the case, and when she realized what it was, she got on the radio and started reporting what she found. By this time, Testo was outside in the airport's parking lot. Two cops came running towards Testo. He shot one in the head, and had a brief shootout with the other. A woman was getting out of her car, and dropped to the ground when she heard the shots fired. Testo grabbed the keys out of her hand and said, "You better move, lady!" The woman went running off screaming as Testo got into her car. Testo slammed on the gas pedal and backed out of the parking space. A bullet shot straight through the window nearly hitting him .Testo looked through the windshield and seen Zig-Zag standing by the exit. Testo then pulled out his gun, and shot out the rest of the windshield. Zig-Zag kept shooting at Testo as the car went speeding across the parking lot. Valhalla and Folks came riding up to Zig-Zag on the Fire Bullets. Zig-Zag got on the back of Valhalla's bike, and they took off after Testo. Testo went speeding onto I-95 , with Folks, Zig-Zag and Valhalla quickly behind him. A caravan of police came speeding down the highway. Testo was now pissed off! He loaded a new clip into his gun and shot at Valhalla. The bullet shot passed her as she quickly swerved out of the way. One of the cops who was in pursuit was struck in the head by a bullet. This caused about six cop cars to crash on the highway. As the dead officer lost control of the car. Folks pulled out a small Uzi, held steady and shot at Testo. The bullets from Folks' gun shot out the back window of Testo's car. Testo turned around, he and Folks locked eyes in hatred for a second. Testo then flung his arm over the back seat of the car and started shooting at Folks. Folks' bike swerved to dodge the bullets. Testo drove straight across two lanes and took an exit to 476. Folks, Zig-Zag and Valhalla followed with no problem, but most of the pursuing officers couldn't make the close turn at the last minute. Testo smashed the gas pedal down and took off like a rocket. Valhalla told Zig-Zag to engage the RPG's. A missile from the side of her Fire Bullet launched and missed Testo's car. Testo looked surprised as hell then fired at Folks until his weapon clicked empty. Testo cursed then threw the gun into the back seat of the car, and took another exit off of 476 . The exit opened up into a neighborhood. Testo almost crashed his car coming around the exit. Zig-Zag came speeding around the exit and pulled out one of the guns that Snipps made for him. He aimed it at the tires of Testo's car. Zig-Zag squeezed the trigger, and in an instant Testo's tires disintegrated. Testo's car swerved, and fishtailed then flipped over smashing into an abandoned house. Smoke and debris were everywhere from the crash. Testo's car was on fire and as the three of them approached the car they noticed there was no sign of movement. Valhalla stopped her bike. Folks stopped his bike, and quickly got off. As he got off the bike the car exploded inside of the house. The three of them fell to the ground in search of cover. A few seconds later Zig-Zag ran up to the porch of the house and looked at the car. Through the flames Zig-Zag could see that Testo was not in the car. Testo was no were to be seen! Valhalla could hear police sirens getting close. She ordered for them to leave. Zig-Zag ran to her bike, and got on the back. Folks was still standing by the porch watching the house and car burn. " Folks, let's go!" ordered Zig-Zag. Folks snapped out of his trance and ran back to his bike then got on. The three of them got away from the burning house just before the cops arrived.

CHAPTER 8

The Connection stood in the headquarters of the 24 Elders. He stood there watching the news of the shootout in which six police officers were hurt, and three were dead. A man appeared in the doorway, and greeted The Connection. "I take it that your already catching up on today's events?" said the man to The Connection.

The Connection just nodded his head. "Where is three the hard way?" asked the man while watching the news report.

The Connection sighed then answered, "They will be here shortly!"

"Well when they do arrive, have Folks come to see the Elders!" said the man.

The Connection was now suspicious. As the man walked away The Connection called out to him, "Jenson! Wait a minute!"

The man stopped in his tracks, but never turned around. "What is this about?" asked The Connection.

Jenson, who never turned around waited a second then answered, "If it were meant for you to know they would have asked for you! Now wouldn't they?!"

"He's a great kid, Jenson!"

"He's a protector, and a prodigy, much more than a kid!" answered Jenson.

"Jenson he would give his life for them in a second! He should know the true origins! Not just about Testo, but about himself!" The Connection demanded.

Jenson smiled with his back still turned towards The Connection then said, "I'll be sure to run that by them. After all, you know what is best!"

Jenson then walked off. The Connection stood motionless, and pissed off for a second. He got himself together then left out off the room.

A guard was coming down the hallway and saw The Connection. "Sir, may I have a word with you?" asked the guard.

"Yes, but let's go to the downstairs office," said The Connection.

When the two men went inside of the office the guard went over to a computer, and began to put in his I. D code. "Sir, I was inside of the archives, and well, see for yourself," said the guard.

The Connection's face went pale as he read what was on the computer. "You did the right thing!" said The Connection. The Connection downloaded the information onto a disk. When the download was finished he snatched the disk out of the computer and left the room.

The Connection made his way to an upstairs room. As he approached the room he heard a voice ask, "Is there something that I can help you with?"

The Connection saw Jenson looking out of the window. "It's imperative that I speak to The Elders this minute!" said The Connection.

"Which star?" Jenson asked.

"All of them!" demanded The Connection.

Jenson turned around and looked at The Connection, smiled and asked, "Are you sure I cant help you?"

"The Elders!" said The Connection.

"Alright, follow me!" said Jenson while looking The Connection up and down.

The Connections face lightened, and he followed the man to a near by room. All 24 Elders were meditating when the two men entered the room. All 24 Elders hovered about three feet off of the ground. "What can I help you with?" asked Star 19.

The Connection started to speak. "With all due respect, sir, I asked Jenson to arrange a meeting with myself, and The Elders a while ago!"

Star 3 spoke. "Mr. Jenson is a busy man, but his intentions are good."

"Is there a problem?" asked Star 6.

"Yes! I request that you inform Folks on the severity off his mission!" The Connection stated.

"You mean tell him that he is destined to die for us?" asked Star 3.

The Connection looked around slowly then said, "Yes!"

"What else can we do for you?" asked Star 5.

The Connection cleared his throat then spoke. "It has been brought to my attention that Testo was once chosen to protect you!"

"This is true!" said Star 3.

The Connection's face was puzzled.

"When Mr. Bell arrives, have him come to see us," said Star 6.

The Connection stood there with more questions bursting to come out of his mouth, but knew it better to make a humble exit. Jenson waved The Connection towards the door. The Connection thanked The Elders for their time, and left the room. Jenson walked The Connection out of the door, and down the hallway. At the end of the hallway Jenson stopped, and said softly, "Have a nice day!"

The Connection paid no attention, and kept walking. As The Connection came downstairs, Zig-Zag, Folks and Valhalla entered the house. "All is well?" asked The Connection.

"Were not dead if that's what you mean!" answered Valhalla.

"Yeah, but Testo's not dead either!" said Folks. The Connection looked at Folks and said, "All in due time, Folks, all in due time!"

Folks just shrugged his shoulders. Folks The Elders would like to speak too," said The Connection.

Tension was in the air, and everyone could feel it! Folks looked at Zig-Zag. "O.k., they want to see me now, or…" Before Folks could finish stalling The Connection spoke up. "Now Folks."

Valhalla looked worried!

Jenson appeared in the doorway and said, "Let's go, Mr. Bell."

The Connection looked at Jenson with hate, and Jenson caught the look. Folks and Jenson left the room. Valhalla quickly moved in front of The Connection and asked, "What is going on!"

The Connection looked at Zig-Zag who also wanted to know what was going on! "Come! I have something to show you two," said The Connection.

The three of them walked off to a room near by. The Connection peeped out of the door to make sure that no one was following them before he closed it. The Connection moved towards a computer and slid the disk in. What came on the screen was something that Valhalla and Zig-Zag wouldn't have expected in a million years. "What the fuck is that! Tell me that's a joke!" demanded Zig-Zag.

Valhalla was god smacked.

"I wish it was a joke," The Connection said.

"So Testo was chosen to work for The Elders before Folks was chosen?" asked Valhalla calmly.

The Connection shook his head, and said, "Yes."

"So let me guess, he turned on them, and now Folks is close to getting his head cut off by this motherfucker?" asked Zig-Zag.

The Connection shook his head in disgust.

"So what are they telling Folks? Are they explaining all of this to him?" asked Valhalla.

The Connection was silent for a second, then said, "I have worse news. Folks must die in the war in order to have The Elders prevail."

Zig-Zag quickly shot back, "He knows how dangerous this war will be, but he'll be fine."

The Connection shook his head, and said, "No Zig-Zag, The Elders said that in order for Testo to die, Folks has to die! For the world to be at peace, Folks must give his life!"

Zig-Zag shook his head slowly.

"But why?" asked Valhalla.

" I don't know!" said The Connection.

Folks looked at Jenson's facial expression as they walked. Jenson's expression was hard to read, but Folks knew that something was wrong. Jenson kept quiet, and so did Folks. When they got to the room, The Elders were still meditating three feet off of the ground. The room had a strong smell of incense. Folks could feel the peace and harmony of the room. Jenson exited the room, closed the door behind him. The Elders were all quiet for a second. Folks just stood their taking in the sights, and atmosphere of the room. After a second, one of The Elders spoke, "How's all, Mr. Folks?"

Folks didn't say anything, but just gave a faint smile towards The Elder. Another one of The Elders began to speak, "Folks, a while ago we asked you what was a righteous man who did not use his righteousness , and you answered NOT RIGHTEOUS. Do you remember that?"

Folks gently nodded his head yes.

"Well Folks he is much more than that! He is in fact the potential devastation of life!" said The Elder.

Another Elder began, "At one time a man was chosen to do the job that you are doing for us now. This man at one point in time was righteous, although he couldn't see that. This man lost his way, and never looked back! That man is Raul Testo!" One-thousand questions ran through Folks' head in an instant, but one came out of his mouth first.

"What turned him?" asked Folks.

"His own will!" said The Elder.

"And now Folks, the question is are you brave enough to fight this war? Up and until this point you have a choice, but after this your time is limited," said The Elder.

Folks thought for a second then said, "This war is personal to me now! Dr. Bright was like my father, and I won't stop until I kill Testo! Besides, I don't think Testo would let me bow out at this point. He would still come after me!"

"You make very strong points, Mr. Folks. There is no lie in you, and there is no quieting with you. You are truly guided by a magnificent spirit!" said The Elder.

After a moment another Elder bluntly said, "Folks, you have to die for us to prevail!"

Folks couldn't believe what he just heard! The room was now spinning in confusion. Before he could speak The Elder continued. "Folks, there has to be a life for a life. A gift given, and a gift taken. If you so choose, you can now turn back. If this is what you want ,Folks, now is the time!"

Folks sighed deeply, and gently walked towards the doors, and opened them. As he walked out he heard The Elder say "now is the time." Jenson was standing outside of the doors. he reached out to close the doors as Folks walked out of them. Jenson closed the doors, and had to fast pace it to catch up with Folks. "Did all go well?" he asked Folks.

"If it didn't, I'm sure its something you cant fix!" Folks said. At that Jenson stopped walking. Folks headed down the steps, and through a door at the bottom of the stairs.

Testo laid fully clothed on a bed in a motel. As he looked up at the ceiling his body shook in pain. Blood ran like a faucet from a gash in the back of his head. He took a deep breath, and got the energy to get himself off of the bed, and onto his feet. Testo then staggered to the bath room, and kneeled down in front of the sink. He stayed like that for a minute, then stood up and looked inside of the medicine cabinet. After finding nothing of use in the cabinet Testo threw the items out, and slammed the doors shut. Feeling a mixture of pain, and anger Testo felt himself losing control. He saw a ^{First Aid} kit on a shelf , and snatched the box. He then sat down on the toilet, and began to search the kit. He pulled a needle and thread out of the kit, and stood up to face the mirror. As he stood up the First Aid kit fell to the floor with the rest off the contents falling out. Testo looked around for a few seconds, and then back in the mirror. He quickly punched the bottom of the mirror, and broke off a hand held piece. He then threaded the needle, and positioned himself with his back against the sink. He held the broken piece of mirror in the air so he could see the back of his head. Testo then began to push the needle through one side of the cut, and pull it through to the other. He did this with one hand at first until he got the hang of it. He then sat the mirror down, and struggled to stitch the rest of his wound. When Testo finished he left out of the bathroom, and sat down on the bed. He sat there with his rage on overdrive. All he could think about was killing Folks. Testo began to glow a bright red while sitting there shaking from hate. All of a sudden Testo jumped up, and punched the wall, and the wall smashed to bits as if a truck hit it!

CHAPTER 9

Folks stood with his guns pointed at the paper target that was about fifty-feet down the range. Folks' emotions ran from hate to fear, and all in between. Zig-Zag was in the next stall also practicing his shooting. Zig-Zag wanted to say something to Folks about the whole situation, but wanted to wait for the right time. The room was deathly quiet as Folks began to shot his gun at the target. BOOM, BOOM, BOOM, BOOM! Folks' rage was boiling at each squeeze of the trigger. Zig-Zag leaned over, and looked at Folks, who was now glowing a bright green color. Folks stood like a soldier, steadfast, and with the look of the devil in his face. Folks was glowing more and more with each squeeze of the trigger. When Zig-Zag looked back at the paper target, all of the shots hit either the head or torso perfectly! Zig-Zag looked back at Folks, and just then Folks' gun clicked empty. Folks stood there, gun still pointed at the target squeezing the trigger. CLICK, CLICK, CLICK. Folks came out of the trance, and stood there holding the pistol as he looked around, and breathed hard. Folks glanced over at Zig-Zag, who had a shocked expression on his face. "You O.K.?" asked Zig-Zag, in a calm voice.

Folks put the gun down, and pressed the button for the paper target to come forward. "That's nice shooting, Tex!" Zig-Zag said to Folks as the target came near.

"Tell me something, Zig-Zag, why do I feel like I'm a good deed done at a bad time?" Folks asked.

"Not a bad time, but a misunderstood time. And definitely not a deed, but a blessing! I don't know of anyone else who would put their life on the line for people they don't even know! Not these days!" SAID Zig-Zag.

"You know what, Zig-Zag, the responsibility of all this strangely completes me. The people needs me, and I need them."

Zig-Zag shook his head gently. "Something just doesn't seem right, Folks. The Connection told us that you must die in order for the world to live. Who am I to question, and maybe I'm biased because it's you, but none of this makes since!" said Zig-Zag.

Folks shook his head lightly, and then sighed. "the story gets deeper, Zig-Zag," Folks began.

Before Folks could finish, Zig- Zag cut in. "Testo was chosen to protect them before you! Makes since as to why The Head Entity was shish-kabobbed to the wall. Testo was using him to get to The Elders all this time!" said Zig-Zag.

"Almost makes me feel sorry for the man," said Folks, sarcastically.

"Fuck him!" Zig-Zag shot back. "He would have sang you the same song, Folks! He may not have been as smart as Testo, but he was damn sure as dangerous!"

Folks agreed with him, then picked the gun back up, and put a new clip in it. "I'll tell you one thing, I'm not going anywhere without the fight of my life!" stated Folks.

"I see that you're getting pretty good at your aim," said Zig-Zag. Folks smiling. "I told you! Things would come naturally, giving the time."

The room was filled with the smell of gun powder and smoke. Just as the smoke started to clear, Folks could see a figure walking towards him. Valhalla came walking out of the smoke. She had the grace and poise of a model as she walked up to Folks and Zig-Zag. "The Connection has a team out and about searching for any signs of Testo" she said.

"Good move on The Connection's part, but if the team does come across Testo, they'll be dead before they know it!" said Zig-Zag.

"Where do you think a deranged scientist turned terrorist would hide out these days?" asked Folks.

"Good question. We could always go and find out!" said Valhalla. Zig-Zag looked at Folks, and gave him a smile.

The Connection walked up the steps to The Elders' floor. When he reached the top Jenson came out of nowhere and asked, "Can I help you?"

"I need to speak to The Elders," said The Connection calmly.

Jenson gave The Connection a smug look, then said, "Follow me!"

The two men went walking down the hall to a room where The Elders were inside. When they reached the room Jenson asked The Connection if everything was O.K. The Connection just smiled. The Connection walked inside of the room, and found that all twenty-four of The Elders were having some sort of conversation about planets, and the life on them. "What of the progress?" asked Star 6.

"Testo is not in custody yet!" I have special teams searching for him now," said The Connection.

"We must move fast! Testo is a very violent man. He could strike at any time!" said Star 3.

"What about Folks? How is all with him?" asked Star 6.

"He's fine," The Connection answered.

The Connection turned to exit the room when Star 6 spoke. "I know you are very fond of him, but fate is fate."

"That's what I'm afraid of!" said The Connection. The Connection thanked The Elders for their time, and assured them that he would keep them posted on all future events. The Connection then exited the room with Jenson behind him. "Just where are the trio?" Jenson asked.

"Out and about, Mr. Jenson," said The Connection. Jenson Smiled. Valhalla led Folks and Zig-Zag to a room with high tech computer equipment.

"So how do we find out where Testo is hiding?" asked Zig-Zag.

Valhalla was pirating about six different police stations. listening to 911 calls .She was listening to anything out of the ordinary. "Well boys, we sit and wait for our name to be called," said Valhalla. Zig-Zag and Folks looked confused. "I'm listening to 911 calls. Sooner or later Testo will do something, and it wont be anything like purse snatching. I'm not looking for the obvious, I'm looking for..." Before Valhalla could finish a call came over the radio from the Upper Darby Police Department. "Officers 829 and 625 report to Baltimore Pike and Church Lane, for a man breaking up one of the motel rooms," announced the dispatcher. "Dispatch, this is Officer Jackson, car 829 is in pursuit."

"Subject checked in yesterday, and started thrashing his room today!" said the dispatcher.

"This is Officer Clinton, car 625. I'm on my way!"

"That's the call, Valhalla!" said Zig-Zag.

"Let's go!" ordered Valhalla. The three of them quickly moved down stairs to The Fire Bullets. Valhalla and Zig-Zag jumped on one of the bikes, with Valhalla driving. Folks jumped onto the other bike, and the trio rode off to their destination.

Officer Jackson pulled into the motel parking lot, with his lights and sirens going. Officer Clinton was about a block away. Officer Jackson could hear yelling and screaming from inside of the motel. The cop drew his weapon from his holster. By this time the second Officer was coming into the parking lot. Officer Jackson ran inside of the motel. The motel keeper met him at the entrance. "This way, Officer! Asshole is tearing up everything!" said the motel keeper. The cops rushed down the corridor to the room.

"He's in there," said the keeper, pointing to a room. The cops could hear furniture smashing, and a man's voice yelling from inside of the room. Officer Clinton stepped to one side of the wall with his gun raised.

Officer Jackson knocked on the door hard. BANG, BANG, BANG! "Open up it's the police! We want to speak to you!" ordered Officer Jackson. All of a sudden the loud noise, and wrecking sound stopped. The two cops looked at each other. Officer Clinton told the motel keeper to get back to her desk, and wait for the other officers to come.

As the keeper went running off, Officer Jackson started banging on the door. "Open up man, we just want to talk to you! Open up or were coming in!" said Officer Clinton.

"No need, I'll come out!" said Testo. Testo broke through the door like an explosion. He grabbed one of the cops, and threw him off of the balcony. The second cop fired and missed Testo's ear by an inch. Testo hit the cop in his stomach, took the gun, and shot the cop as he fell to the ground. Testo then jumped off of the balcony. More cops were coming into the parking lot. Testo was now glowing red.

"Drop the weapon, and put up your hands!" ordered an officer. Test stood there for a few seconds. "Sir, put the weapon down!" ordered the officer.

"You're prey to me!" Testo whispered. Testo then sprung into action, and jumped off of the balcony. He leapt over a near by car. The cops started shooting, and filled the car that Testo hide behind with bullets. Testo stayed down for a second.

"Cease fire, cease fire!" yelled one of the officers. The shooting stopped, and all was quiet. Testo, now glowing red, and furious smacked the car that he was hiding behind. The bullet riddled car flew about 20 feet, and smashed into several cops. The officers that were still standing, turned and looked at the wreck behind them. The officers turned back around, and started shooting again. Testo quickly jumped behind a wall. The cops bullets eat away chunks of the wall in no time. Testo came from around the walls, and started shooting at the cops. Two of the cops were hit immediately. Testo started to move towards the cops while shooting. He tossed another car which flew into the parked police cars. Testo ran past the officers, and the wreckage and out of the parking lot. As Testo ran down the street he heard the hiss of a missile. Testo turned around, and saw a rocket headed towards him. Testo side stepped the missile, and looked at the trio that he hated so much in the distance. Testo stood there for a second, controlled his breathing, and took off towards off towards the three like a bolt of lightening. Valhalla launched another missile at Testo which he also dodged. Testo moved back and forth in fast streaks while dodging bullets at the same time. As Testo got close to them, Folks stopped his bike, and got off. Folks started running towards Testo, equally as fast. Testo jumped into the air, and was coming down towards Zig-Zag and Valhalla. As they braced for impact, Folks now glowing green, hit Testo full blast by running into him with a bone crushing force that would make any football tackle look weak. Testo flew into a parked car, and smashed the whole side of it in. Folks started moving towards Testo who was getting off of the ground. "You fucking bitch!" said Testo shaking his head slowly. Testo then started to run towards Folks. The two smashed into each other like fighting Mack trucks. Valhalla and Zig-Zag were now off of the Fire Bullet, and in awe as to what they were seeing. After a second, Zig-Zag began shooting at Testo. Testo pushed away from Folks, and jumped back as the bullets flew by. Testo ran towards Zig-Zag while dodging bullets, and grabbed Zig-Zag by the neck then threw him about ten feet away. Zig-Zag fell to the street. When he looked up Testo was walking towards him. Zig-Zag looked over, and seen his guns about four feet away. Zig-Zag quickly moved towards the gun. Folks hit Testo in his face, and again Testo went flying into the street. Cops were now speeding towards the scene by the dozens. Folks moved toward Zig-Zag to make sure he was o.k. Testo now closer to Zig-Zag's gun than he, grabbed the gun, and started shooting. Folks and Zig-Zag moved out of the way, and a bullet hit Valhalla who was standing behind them. Valhalla hit the ground in an instant as Testo took off running. Folks looked at Testo, and decided it would be better not to chase after him. Valhalla's condition was much more important to him now. "She's hit in the shoulder, Folks!" yelled Zig-Zag. Folks got on the Fire Bullet with Valhalla sitting in front facing Folks. She was bleeding bad as she slumped over, and laid on Folks' chest. Zig-Zag jumped on his bike, and the three of them took off.

CHAPTER 10

Folks laid in his bed, tossing and turning. He couldn't get his mind off of Valhalla. The Elders Dr. had worked on Valhalla, and removed the bullet. Folks wanted to kill Testo more than ever, even it would cost him his life in the process. After a while Folks became still, and started to fade off into sleep. Just then Folks was in the middle of a rain storm. He stood there trying to figure out where he was. As Folks looked up in the sky lightning struck in the air. A beautiful, but dangerous streak of colors went flashing through the air. Folks turned around, and walked off. Just then a second bolt of lightning struck the ground about thirty feet away from Folks. He just stood there wondering what was going on. A third bolt of lightning then struck the ground twenty feet behind him. Folks turned around on his heels very fast towards the bolt of lighting . Standing in the spot of the bolt was a young boy. "Who is that?" Folks demanded to know. When the young boy heard that he stepped forth, and Folks could see that it was The Son of Lilith. Folks stood there looking at the boy, and remembering how Zig-Zag told him that the boy was dangerous.

"Hello," the boy simply said.

Folks couldn't wait to find out what the boy wanted from him. "Hello," Folks said in a whisper.

"I have been waiting for you. It's very impressive to see how righteous you are, Mr. Folks," said the boy. Folks just listened. The boy continued in his angelic voice. "Testo is a great threat to you, and Earth weeps because she feels that you death is near. A whole lot of people will lose out then!" The boy shook his head slowly, and looked down at the ground. Folks listened passionately. He couldn't believe that this was a small boy who was talking to him. The boy seemed more like an adult to Folks. "I could kill Testo for you, Mr. Folks," said the boy, still looking at the ground. Folks couldn't believe what he had just heard the boy say.

"What makes you think that I need you? What makes you think that Testo will kill me?" asked Folks.

"What makes Earth think that Testo will kill you!?" asked the boy. Folks was at a loss for words. So many thoughts was running through his mind it left him speechless. "You have to know when to gracefully bow out, if not it may get you killed!" the boy said strongly.

"What's in it for you?" Folks asked.

"I like doing favors for people!" stated the boy. Folks was not convinced, and the boy knew it. "Mr. Folks if I kill Testo, you have to bow down to me! If you bow down to me I want the information on The Elders so I can destroy them, and I want to destroy them!" said the boy.

"I think I'll take the chance on myself," Folks said.

As the rain poured down heavily, lightning started to flash in the sky again. "Or will you!?" asked the boy sternly. Lightning struck near the boy, and illuminated his face. Folks could now see that this was no boy. His eyes showed that the boy was pure evil. Evil that the world has never seen, and never wants to see. The boy stepped closer towards Folks. As he did so, two lions came out of nowhere, rushed past Folks, and stopped, then just stared at the boy. The boy stopped, and looked at Folks then smiled. "You didn't tell me we had company," said the boy slowly. Lightning then struck, and illuminated the thousands of demon like creatures that were under the boys rule. "TAP TAP!" commanded the boy. The army stood at attention. The two lions growled, and stood alert. Folks and the boy looked eyes as lightning now flashed around violently, and the rain poured down extremely heavy. As a war was silently beginning. Folks could hear weeping in the distance behind him. All eyes, even those of the lions, turned to see Earth's small body in the near distance. Crying and sobbing harder, and harder. Folks was furious, but remained still. The lightning seemed to dissipate as Earth spoke. "How many souls do you own, your flesh and blood is now their home, the righteous wont bow, and yet somehow, you feel it threatens your throne." All was quiet! Folks looked at the boy, who tossed his head back to move his long hair out of his face.

The boy then looked at Folks. "Guard down!" the boy order to his army. The boy's army stood at ease. "Move out!" ordered the boy. The army turned around, and marched off. The boy gave one last glare at Folks then opened his bat like wings, and took off into the rainy night. The lions calmly walked off. When Folks turned to look for Earth, she was gone. All that was left was a single red rose lying on the ground. Folks heard Earth's voice softly say, "Keep believing, Folks, nothing is written in stone. Your fate is just that. YOUR fate!"

Folks picked up the rose as the words from Earth's soft voice stuck in his mind.

Folks' eyes popped open as he lay in his bed. His heart was racing as he wondered if it was a dream or not. He jumped out of bed, and quickly moved towards a window in his room. In the moonlight distance he could see The Son of Lilith and his army moving into the night. Just then it was a knock at Folks' door. Folks walked over to the door, and flung it wide open. Standing there was Zig-Zag. He was surprised to see Folks sweating, and glowing green. "Is all okay?" asked Zig-Zag.

Folks nodded his head yes. "Valhalla's awake. She's doing good, and asked me to come get you, and bring you to see her," Zig-Zag told Folks.

Folks grabbed a shirt, and the two men moved downstairs to where Valhalla was resting. Folks was furious, and Zig-Zag could tell. "Not resting well?" asked Zig-Zag.

"I just want this thing to be over!" said Folks.

"Over!?" asked Zig-Zag bluntly.

Folks just looked at Zig-Zag. "What are you saying?" asked Zig-Zag.

"I'm just saying it is me he wants….maybe I should just let him…."

Zig-Zag cut Folks off from talking. "Valhalla is getting shot! Then she wakes up, and the first person she asks for is you! I'm doing everything in my power, The Connection is fighting The Elders tooth and nail for you, and you standing here telling me that your plotting on giving up! What do you think happens if he kills you? Do you think were safe? Do you think the world would be safe? That motherfucker is coming for us! Shit! I'm fighting that bastard! I'm fighting that bastard until I get my wings, or until I'm banished to hell! You need to make up your mind right now! You going to die or survive!? Because waiting around for Testo to write you're ending ain't going to work!"

Zig-Zag stepped closer to Folks, and with a snarl in his voice said, "Folks, I know that you're stronger than this. What's the problem?"

Without thinking Folks shoved Zig-Zag up against a wall, and looked him in his eyes then said, "You heard what The Elders said! The Connection told you! A life for a life! Mine. A few weeks ago I was regular old me. Now I giving my life for the world! I run around all of the time, chasing a crazy man who's got fucking earthquake machines. My mentor, and best friend was blown up in his house! What the hell am I supposed to do? How the hell am I supposed to feel? You tell me! What's left?"

Zig-Zag looked at Folks for a second, and calmly took Folks' hands off of himself. "We're left! Me, Valhalla and The Connection. You're left!" said Zig-Zag calmly.

Folks stood there with a serious, but apologetic look on his face. "One thing I believe is that your future is not written. It's always room for change in everyone's life. Folks, I don't believe that you have to die. Something tells me that you can win. I know it. I feel in my heart that we can win, and I don't give a shit what The Elders told you!" said Zig-Zag. Zig-Zag turned and looked up at a staircase that was over top of him and Folks. "Jenson!" Zig-Zag yelled out. A second later Jenson appeared at the banister of the staircase, and looked down on the two men. "You can tell them how I feel, you understand me?" ordered Zig-Zag.

Jenson gave a half smile and said, "I think that they are aware, Mr. Zig- Zag."

Zig-Zag just looked at Jenson. A second later Jenson walked off. Folks and Zig-Zag proceeded to a room where Valhalla was resting.

Testo was hiding in an abandoned barn deep in Bucks County, Pennsylvania. In the barn he found a small generator, some metal and tools. The dress shirt that he wore was ripped and torn. The roof of the barn was half gone, and all of the windows were broken out. Testo was welding two flat pieces of metal together in a square shape as if he was making a box. Sparks flew everywhere as Testo welded piece after piece of metal together. His hand were covered with little burn marks from the sparks of the blowtorch. "Folks Bell! I'm going to fucking kill you!" Testo said to himself.

The Connection was in the room with Valhalla when Folks and Zig-Zag came in. "Hey you," said Zig-Zag

Valhalla smiled. Folks looked at her and tried to smile but settled on lowering his head to the ground. Valhalla look at Folks for a few seconds then spoke. "Hey." Folks kept looking at the ground. "Hey," Valhalla said a little louder. Folks now looked up at her. "I'm still here," said Valhalla.

How can she look so beautiful while lying in the bed with a gunshot wound Folks wondered. "Hey! Are you o.k.?" Valhalla asked Folks again.

"He's fine. He'll be fine," Zig-Zag answered.

"Gentlemen, can I talk to Folks in private for a second?" asked Valhalla.

Both Zig-Zag and The Connection agreed, and quietly left out of the room. Valhalla waited for the door to close before she spoke. "So how are you?" Valhalla asked.

Folks managed to fake a half decent smile. "Listen Valhalla, I'm sorry for all of this. I never meant to get you hurt," said Folks in a soft voice.

Valhalla looked at Folks for a second softly then answered, "You didn't get me hurt! And It's not your fault."

"But if I…" Folks tried to speak, but was cut off by Valhalla.

"No buts, Folks. If it wasn't for you, I wouldn't be alive now." Valhalla sighed, and then said, "We are all doing our best to control this situation, and bring Testo down. There's no reason to take the blame for anything, Folks." Valhalla looked at Folks, and could tell that he was feeling better from their conversation. "Is Folks concerned with me?" asked Valhalla in a joking manner. The two of them laughed. "Folks, I don't care what they tell you about you're fate. Listen to your heart! It's the best voice for you," said Valhalla. Valhalla laid back in her bed. "When I get better I'm paying Testo back triple!" she said.

Folks smiled at her courage, and walked over to the door. "Get some rest, and I'll check on you later," Folks said.

"I've known Zig-Zag for a long time. He has been waiting to meet you Folks. He and Dr. Bright were the first ones to believe in you," said Valhalla.

Folks gave her a smile, and walked out of the room. Folks went to another room. The Connection and Zig-Zag sat at a computer. Folks noticed that the two men were very interested in what was on the monitor. A steady radar like sound could be heard. BEEP, BEEP, BEEP. The two men were tracking something, and by the determined looks on their faces Folks knew exactly who. "How did you get a track on him?" asked Folks as he walked to the desk where the men were seated.

"The last time we had lunch with Testo, I managed to slip a tiny GPS tracker into his back. Snipps made these cool B.B. sized trackers that latch onto your target undetected," Zig-Zag answered. Folks was impressed especially since he had no clue that Zig-Zag had done this.

"Where is he now?" asked Folks.

"He's in Bucks County," said The Connection.

"And where're not on our way because...?" Folks asked in a sarcastic tone of voice.

"Naw. Let's get a good jump on him. Let's see what's going on," said Zig-Zag.

" Testo is out not out there to hide. He's working on something. Let's see what it is!" said The Connection.

The Son of Lilith stood on the other side of the farm in the dark night. He stood there staring into the abandoned barn that Testo was inside of some three-hundred yards away. Testo could feel someone looking at him. The hair on the back of his neck stood up. Slowly Testo turned around, and saw the boy standing there. Although the boy was at least three-hundred yards away he could see and hear Testo as if he was right in front of him. Testo squinted, and his mouth turned to a snarl as he stood there looking at the boy. "What you got there?" asked the boy. Test tightened his jaw at the question. "Looks dangerous!" said the boy with a smile on his face. Testo relaxed his face, but he still had the look of the devil in his eyes. He was fairly surprised that he could see and hear the boy as if he was in front of him, but in fact the boy was so far away. "You think you can beat him?" asked the boy with excitement in his voice.

"What's your business here!" asked Testo.

"Just admiring," said the boy. Testo stood there studying the boy. He knew that the boys army was very near. This helped him remain calm, and it also bought him some time. "So....What are you making there?" asked the boy.

"A machine!" said Testo.

" Gonna have them raging against the machine. Huh?" the boy asked slyly. Testo kept quiet. "Fine with me! I never cared much for this world anyway. Bunch of prey. Ever the predators! They kill their young, and wonder why the future is this way!" said the boy. Testo never took his eyes off of the boy. He stood there hating the boy, but silently agreeing with him, and the words that he spoke. "Tap-Tap!" commanded the boy. Testo heard the army come to attention in the near darkness. He couldn't see the army, but their presence was undeniable. "Anyway, good luck with your machines!" stated the boy. Just then lightning struck around ten feet or so from the barn. Testo quickly turned his head into the direction of the lightning. When he turned back towards the boy, he was gone! Just like that.

Folks sat at the computer table tracking Testo's movements. Testo hadn't moved yet, and Folks never took his eyes off of the screen. Zig-Zag was pacing back and forth like a caged animal. The Connection sat there in deep thought. After a few seconds The Connection came out of his trance. "Zig-Zag! Have a seat please. That's not healthy!" the Connection said.

"Last thing that I'm concerned with is health!" said Zig-Zag.

"Patience, Zig-Zag. That is the key right now," said The Connection.

Zig-Zag stopped pacing, and sat down. "Are you sure we cant go to the local, and blow him the fuck up?" he asked impatiently.

The Connection smiled for a second, then cleared his throat. "He's not out in the middle of nowhere for just any reason. Trust me, Zig-Zag. He would know that we were coming a mile away!" said The Connection.

Zig-Zag looked sick as he sat there starting to see The Connection's point. The radar started to beep faster. "He's on the move!" said Folks with excitement.

Zig-Zag rushed over to the table. The Connection stood up, and focused on the computer also. "He's moving towards the city!" said Zig-Zag.

"Track him!?" Folks asked Zig-Zag.

"Track him!" said Zig-Zag.

A long shiny 1963 black Cadillac calmly rolled down route 309 towards Philadelphia. Inside was Raul Testo. As his driver kept a steady, fast pace as Testo sat in the back seat gently tapping his fingers on the metal box. Testo's face showed extreme impatience. His mind was made up, and he couldn't wait to show the world what he thought.

Valhalla came strolling into the room where Folks and Zig-Zag were. The two men were picking out guns and ammo for their outing. Zig-Zag looked up, and saw Valhalla standing there. Folks turned to see what Zig-Zag was looking at, and saw Valhalla. She stood there looking at the two men with their guns in hand. "Party tonight, fellas, and you didn't invite me?" she asked.

Folks smiled. Zig-Zag passed Valhalla a holster with two small Uzi's strapped to it. "You're all set to paint the town red my lady," said Zig-Zag.

"Thank ya, thank ya," said Valhalla as she grabbed a hold of the holster, and quickly twirled it around her shoulders. The tracking device started to beep again. "What's that?" asked Valhalla.

"That's Testo. I'm tracking him from Bucks County. The closer he gets to us, the more it beeps," said Zig-Zag

"Great, so when do we leave?" asked Valhalla.

"Not until morning. Gives us distance, and I'm curious to see where he goes," said Zig-Zag. Folks picked up his small bag of guns, Zig-Zag picked up his. The trio then made their way upstairs to The Connection. The Connection sat talking to one of The Elders when the trio came into the room. The Elder and The Connection stood up. Folks put the bag of guns on one of the tables in the room, and started to crack his neck by moving it in side-to-side motions. Zig-Zag and Valhalla just stood there quiet, but right next to Folks.

The Elder looked the trio up and down with a look of approval on his face then spoke. "I believe in the three of you, and I wanted to personally thank you. The world is not a perfect place. It's an everyday struggle, but if it is true that only the strong shall survive then you three will be fine until the end of time. I understand that you're tracking Testo, and ready to move soon. To that I say great luck, and God speed!"

The three said nothing, but pride and appreciation was in their eyes. The Elder looked at Folks, and gave him a nod on his way out of the room. Folks just looked over into The Connection's direction with a "what is this about!" look on his face. The Elder calmly walked out of the door to an awaiting Jenson in the hallway. Jenson and Zig-Zag caught eyes before the door shut, and Jenson flashed him a sly smile. "You see that shit!?" Zig-Zag asked Valhalla.

"Let it go!" she said.

"How do you feel, Valhalla?" asked The Connection.

"Back to me!" she answered.

The Connection smiled then looked at Folks and Zig-Zag. "You two got everything that you need?" asked The Connection.

"We should be good!" said Zig-Zag.

CHAPTER II

Folks sat in his bedroom that night gazing out of the window, and looking up at the stars. He forgot how beautiful they were. He couldn't sleep, but that wasn't from nervousness. Folks was at peace with what may be in front of him. For once in his life he actually believed in himself and his fate. Whether it be good or bad. He thought back to the first night that all of this started. How Dr. Bright came into the observatory that rainy night. He thought about how never in a million years did he think that the present night would come out of a stormy evening. The GPS device started to beep, and broke Folks' concentration. He stood up, and walked over to it. When he picked it up and looked at it, it showed Testo's location as being in a place just off of 17th and Chestnut Street, in Philadelphia. With all of the high-rise buildings in that area, it made Folks very uneasy to think about how many people that Testo could hurt, or worse! Folks put the GPS tracker back on the table, and was a little startled to see Earth standing there with a small model of the planets in her hands. "Is this yours, Folks?" she asked.

Folks was shocked for a second, and then said, "Yes. A very special friend gave that to me."

"You mean Dr. Bright," Earth said with a smile. Folks smiled back at Earth.

"This is such a nice model that you have here, Folks."

Folks smiled again. Pointing to Earth on the model, Earth said, "Look, Earth," and smiled at Folks.

"Listen Folks, you came a long way. Keep believing. I don't care what anyone told or what anyone said, keep believing. Nothing is written in stone!" she said.

Folks shook his head slowly, and agreed with her. "Thank you, Earth. For everything!" he said. Earth smiled really big, and handed Folks the model of the planets. Folks gently took the model out of Earth's small hands.

Early the next morning, Folks' eyes popped open to the sound of the GPS. Testo was very close, and now was the moment of truth. Folks jumped up quick, and moved to the bathroom. As Folks was washing his face he heard a knock at the door. "Yes?" Folks said.

The door opened, and in came Zig-Zag. "Ready?" he asked Folks.

After a few seconds Folks looked at Zig-Zag and said, "More than!"

Zig-Zag nodded his head in approval. "We'll be downstairs," said Zig-Zag.

"I'll be down in ten minutes," said Folks.

Zig-Zag turned to walk out of the door. "Zig-Zag, get the guns, and put them in the car!" ordered Folks. Zig-Zag could tell that Folks was in a "no playing" mode. Very understandable. Considering the day ahead of him. Zig-Zag took the two duffel bags of guns off of the floor, and exited the room. Folks turned off the water, and came out of the bathroom. He stood there looking at a beautiful gray suit hanging on the closet door.

Zig- Zag came down the steps, and saw Valhalla and The Connection loading duffel bags of guns into the trunk of a new all black Mercedes 600. Valhalla looked up, and saw Zig-Zag coming down the steps. She tapped The Connection, who was still loading a bag into the trunk, on the arm. The Connection looked up, and sow Zig-Zag coming down the stairs without Folks. "Where is he!?" The Connection asked frantically.

Zig-Zag calmly walked past The Connection, and threw the bags into the trunk. "He's coming," said Zig-Zag.

"How is he?" Valhalla asked softly. Zig-Zag just gave a fake smile.

"You look great!" said Valhalla.

Zig-Zag was dressed in an all black suit, black shirt and tie, and a black fedora hat. "Thank you. You look great too," Zig-Zag said with a smile.

Valhalla hit Zig-Zag on the arm with a playful tap. "Don't get funny!" said Valhalla, who was dressed in a SEPTA bus drivers uniform.

"No really. You make it work!" said Zig-Zag while smiling.

"I do make it work don't I?" asked Valhalla.

"If you two are finished I would like to know what is going on with him!" said The Connection.

Zig-Zag's face became somber. "He seems fine. I can't read him," said Zig-Zag. The Connection looked at his watch while Zig-Zag started the car.

Folks stood looking into the mirror in his room. Folks was sharp dressed in a gray suit, and a maroon button down dress shirt. The room was silent as he stood there looking into the mirror. He thought about what Earth told him, "Keep believing!" It kept shooting through his mind like a bullet. He dropped his eyes to the ground for a second, and then snapped them back up to eye level of the mirror. Folks was now ready.

The Connection was just about to explode when Folks came down the stairs. "Are you ready?" The Connection managed to ask.

Folks looked The Connection in his eyes and said, "More than!"

The Connection smiled, and then put his hand on Folks' shoulder and said, "You keep strong no matter what! Do you understand?"

"I will," Folks answered while looking The Connection in his eyes. The Connection put his hand out, and Folks shook his hand with a firm grip. "Thank you!" said Folks.

The Connection shook his head with a smile on his face and said, "No Folks. Thank you!"

Testo stood out front of a skyscraper on 17th and Market Street. He stood there looking up at the top of the building as the wind blew past, flinging his tie over his left shoulder. Testo had the most wicked smile on his face as he slowly shook his head, and began to enter the building.

BEEP, BEEP, BEEP, BEEP, BEEP, BEEP!!! Zig-Zag's GPS was now going crazy. "Testo is in a building on 17th and Market," said Zig-Zag looking at Folks.

"What do you think it is, a bomb?" asked Valhalla.

"It's an earthquake machine," Folks said.

"How do you know that?" asked The Connection.

"I just do!" Folks answered.

Five minutes later, the Mercedes pulled up to the corner of 18th and Market Street. Valhalla got out, and casually walked over to a waiting septa bus. She got on, and sat down in the drivers seat. The Mercedes pulled back into traffic, and made a right at 17th and Market. Testo got on an elevator, and pushed the button for the 74th floor. An older woman got on, and asked him to push the 16th floor. Testo pushed the button, and smiled at the woman as she said thank you. Behind Testo was a balding man on a cell phone wearing a black suit, and a white shirt. "Wait, hold on! Hey you!" the man said to Testo. "Push button 54!" said the man.

Testo turned, and pushed the 54th floor button. The man continued to speak into the cell phone. "Listen asshole! Have the reports ready! I'm on the elevator so you have one fucking minute!" said the man. The man then slid the cell phone into his pocket. The woman got off at the 16th floor, and smiled at Testo. The elevator doors closed. Testo pulled out two handguns with silencers, and shot the man several times killing him. Testo then put his right foot on top of the dead man's head, pulled out a handkerchief, and began to wipe the blood off of his shoes as the elevator went upwards.

Testo then pushed a button on the panel that said, "Straight through, no stops." The elevator reached the 74th floor. Testo pushed the emergency brake button, and got off. He looked around to make sure that all was clear. He walked over to a large window that looked out over 17th and Market Street. Testo could see that a large crowd was gathered on the corner. Something wasn't right! Testo looked straight ahead, and could see a police helicopter headed towards the building. He couldn't believe what he was seeing! He looked back down at the street, and could see police cars coming from everywhere. Testo turned around with the earthquake machine under his arm, and headed back to the elevator. He pulled the dead man out of the car, and pushed "L" for lobby. When the elevator reached the bottom floor Testo stood there for a second before he got off.

People inside of the building were being escorted out, so Testo figured that he slip out with them. He quickly walked towards the front door. He heard one of the cops tell someone that it has been a bomb threat. Testo walked across the huge lobby headed towards the doors He reached the middle of the lobby when he heard a voice ask, "First the bomb threat, now me! This is not your lucky day now is it?"

Testo turned, and saw two men sitting on a chaise. One of the men wore a black suit, with his head down, and hidden under a fedora hat. Sitting next to him was the man who spoke. The man was sitting with a newspaper fully open, and Testo couldn't see his face. Although Testo couldn't see the men's faces he knew exactly who it was and pulled a 9 mm and began shooting at the men. Zig-Zag stood up, and started shooting back. Testo ran behind a pillar to take cover. Zig-Zag also ran behind a pillar. Folks took cover behind a wall. He couldn't see Testo, but he could see Zig-Zag. Zig-Zag shot at Testo twice, and hit the pillar. Testo darted out from behind the pillar, and ran towards a large glass window. He fired twice, and broke the window out. Testo jumped through the window, and ran into the middle of Market Street. Folks and Zig-Zag ran after him. The Downtown Center City Street was filled with cars and buses. A man slammed on his brakes just short of hitting Testo. Testo grabbed the man, and threw him out of the car. The man hurled to the ground face first as Testo got into the car, and pulled off. Zig-Zag ran out of the building to the car that The Connection was waiting in. At the same time, Folks came running out of the building with a gun in both hands. He couldn't get clear aim on Testo. Folks started running down the middle of Market Street after Testo. Zig- Zag and The Connection was shocked to see Folks chasing Testo on foot. Folks was to go to the car if Testo exited the building. "Where the fuck is he going?" asked Zig-Zag.

"Let's get him!" The Connection replied. They sped down Market Street towards City Hall. Police were everywhere.

Valhalla sat in the driver's seat of the SEPTA bus at Broad and Market Streets when her phone rang. "Hello," she answered. The people were wondering why she was just sitting there, and they were starting to get agitated about it.

"Valhalla, Testo is headed your way, and so is Folks. He's on foot chasing Testo," Zig-Zag said into the phone.

"Got it!" Valhalla said. She looked into the side mirror of the bus, and could see Testo speeding up the street towards her. Valhalla picked up the microphone, and politely asked the passengers to exit the bus. The passengers kept complaining, and no one moved. Valhalla then drew her gun, and pointed it at the ceiling of the bus. She shot twice while opening the bus' doors. "Everybody off the bus!" she yelled. The passengers raced off of the bus, all except one elderly lady who was moving faster than she had in forty -five years. "You too, granny!" Valhalla said. The elderly lady finally got off of the bus. "Forgive me," Valhalla said as she looked up to the sky, and smiled. Testo came driving past Valhalla. Folks came running down the street, and passed her too. She began to pull out into traffic to join the pursuit. Testo went speeding around City Hall. As he got around the side of City Hall, he lost control of the car and crashed into the front window of a fifty-five story building. Glass, smoke and metal was everywhere. When Folks got to the crash site he could see Testo rip the driver's side door off of the car, and exit the vehicle. Testo then moved further inside of the building. Folks entered the building with a gun in hand. "Folks, wait!" Zig-Zag yelled as he and The Connection came to a screeching halt.

CHAPTER 12

Testo ran to the other end of the lobby, and put the earthquake machine on the ground behind a stone pillar. The people inside of the building looked on in awe. "Where you gonna go?" asked Folks.

Testo's back was turned towards Folks. Testo began to twist and crack his neck without ever turning around to face Folks. "You're right! I guess it's no need to run now," Testo said. Testo started to glow a bright red. He pulled out his gun, and tossed it to the ground. By now people were running out of the building, and police sirens could be heard. Testo stopped cracking his neck. He let out an earsplitting scream, turned towards Folks, and charged at him. Folks was now glowing a bright green. He calmly waited, and when Testo got close Folks punched him with the force of a truck. Testo flew back 15 feet, and crashed through a stone pillar. Folks now went charging towards Testo. Testo jumped up, and kicked Folks, sending him through a pillar. The cops were starting to storm through the door. Testo picked up a large piece of the pillar, and sent it hurling towards the cops, crushing them. Testo walked over to Folks, and picked him up off of the ground by his neck. Folks sent a bone crushing hand chop down on Testo's right shoulder followed by another strong blow to the middle of his chest. Testo let go of Folks, and hit him in the face with the palm of his hand sending Folks stumbling back a few steps. Before Folks could fall to the ground Testo ran at him, and crashed into him with his shoulder. Both off them went smashing into another pillar reducing it to a pile of large rocks. Folks took one of the rocks, and smashed it down on Testo's back. He then grabbed Testo up by the back of his neck, and slammed him to the ground face first. Folks then kicked Testo sending him about 20 feet through the air. Testo smashed into an escalator destroying it. Folks ran to one of the smashed pillars. He picked up a large piece of it, and hurled it at Testo. Testo smashed through it. Folks and Testo ran at each other. Folks hit Testo in the face. Testo blocked the punch, and hit Folks in his chest. Folks took his hands, and crashed down on Testo's ears causing Testo's equilibrium to become off. Folks took advantage of this, and jumped back then kicked Testo. He then kicked Testo again. Testo flew up into the air, and landed on his back causing a large hole around his body in the beautiful white marble floor. Folks picked up another piece of the pillar, and smashed it down on Testo. Testo pushed off of the ground, and smashed through the piece of stone like it was glass. He grabbed Folks by his waist, and threw him to the ground.

Testo was now over the top of Folks, and began to punch him viciously in his face. Zig-Zag began shooting at Testo from a side glass panel that he had broken out. Testo dodged the bullets, and ran. Zig-Zag came through the window shooting at Testo. Testo hid behind one of the last pillars that was standing. Zig-Zag's bullets tore into the pillar with force. When his guns clicked empty Zig-Zag ran over to Folks, and knelt down beside him. "FOLKS!" yelled Zig-Zag. Before Zig-Zag knew it Testo ran over, and kicked him in the side. Zig-Zag went flying out of a large window, and onto the sidewalk. Valhalla came running through the front door full speed, and jumped into the air while firing two guns at Testo. Two bullets hit Testo, one in the left shoulder, and the other in the right leg. Testo managed to dodge the rest of Valhalla's bullets. Valhalla came down to the ground. Testo was glowing bright red. "You fucked up, girl!" Testo snarled as he threw a punch which Valhalla blocked. Testo threw another punch that hit Valhalla in her face. Her guard dropped, and Testo kicked her, sending her flying back out of the building.

As Testo spun around, Folks met him with a kick to his face then a punch to his chest. Folks was glowing a bright green. His teeth snarled like a wolf, and his eyes were as dangerous as a lion. Testo fell back. Before he hit the ground, Folks grabbed him, and threw him about 20 feet into the last standing pillar of the front lobby. Testo laid on the ground for a second. As he started to get up off of the ground, he saw the earthquake machine about three-feet away from him. Testo jumped for the machine, and quickly pressed the "power" button. Folks gave Testo a powerhouse kick to his ribs. A second later the entire ground and building started shaking. The enormous crowd that gathered outside started running in a panic. A helicopter was in the process of dispatching a SWAT team to the roof of the tall building when it collapsed in. The SWAT team fell with the concrete and steel. All except one that was still attached to the rope of the helicopter. "What the fuck!" said one of the helicopter operators.

"GO! GO! GO!" yelled the other.

The helicopter flew away with the SWAT member still dangling from the rope. The crowd was running in panic. The tall building fell inward with great force. Folks moved through the falling debris as if it was raindrops, glowing green as he made his way towards Testo. Testo was guarding the machine like a lion. Stalking back and forth in front of the machine as the ground shook violently under his feet. Helicopters were now in the air by the dozens. Army tanks rolled the streets as soldiers sectioned off a mile long perimeter , and controlled the crowd. The Connection stood in sheer terror as he watched, and wondered what the outcome of this would be. Zig-Zag moved towards The Connection. People were running in a panic, like rats in a snake's cage. Zig-Zag grabbed The Connection by the arm. "Hey, snap out of it!" Zig-Zag said.

"The Elders did not lie, Zig-Zag. They kept their word. Folks shall perish, in order for them to live!" said The Connection.

"Not if I have anything to do with it!" said Zig-Zag.

"Let's get Valhalla!" ordered The Connection.

Zig-Zag and The Connection made their way through the panic stricken crowd. Zig-Zag was scanning the crowd for Valhalla when he spotted something on top of another building. Zig-Zag saw that it was The Son of Lilith, and his army was lined up around the edges of the building. All of the buildings were covered with the boy's army. The boy met Zig-Zag's eye with a smile, and a wave. "Are you surprised to see him?" asked The Connection.

Zig-Zag looked puzzled. "Well you shouldn't be! They're vultures waiting for their pick," said The Connection as he nodded his head to the boy. The boy kept smiling. Zig-Zag spotted Valhalla, and he and The Connection moved towards her.

"Folks is still inside!" said Valhalla. The building was now filly collapsed. Metal, dust and debris was everywhere.

CHAPTER 13

The ground was still shaking as the smoke cleared. The building that Folks and Testo were in was now torn down to its foundation. The ground around the building opened up swallowing the steel and concrete that fell from the building. The ground that the foundation was on resembled an island. The ground that Folks and Testo were on, and past that was what appeared to be an extremely deep pit, that circled the foundation of the building. Testo jumped up from under a pile of rocks. He looked around wildly for Folks. Testo couldn't see Folks anywhere. Just then, a metal beam came crashing down on Testo's back. Testo stumbled forward, and went down on his hands and knees. Testo turned around only to have the metal beam hit him across the face. As Testo laid on his back looking up at the sky, Folks came down with the beam aimed at Testo's head. Testo suddenly rolled to his side, and dodged the blow. Testo jumped to his feet, and kicked at Folks. Folks blocked the kick, and swung the metal beam at Testo. The ground was shaking so hard now that Folks couldn't steady his aim, and he missed. Testo then hit Folks in his stomach, and Folks dropped the beam. Testo hit Folks again, knocking him about ten feet back. Testo moved over to Folks as he was getting off of the ground, and kicked him in his chest. Folks crumbled over in pain as Testo reared back, and kicked him in his face. Folks shook off the kick, and lunged towards Testo. Testo grabbed Folks, and flung him to the ground. Folks hit the ground hard.

A large crack started to form in the street. The people were falling down, and getting trampled from the running crowd. The foundation that Folks and Testo were on was starting to crack also. Testo stood over Folks. He was glowing red, and snarling as he grabbed Folks by the front of his shirt. Testo held Folks in the air as if he was a rag doll. Folks came to, and kicked Testo in his chest. Testo dropped Folks, who then got up off of the shaking ground, and hit Testo in his neck, then kicked him in his face. Folks steadied himself on the shaky ground. As he did, he saw the earthquake box laying on the ground about 15 feet away from him. Folks now glowing green, and mad as hell, stood there for a second, then let Testo get off of the ground. As Testo stood up Folks met him with a powerful kick. Testo shook off the hit, looked over, and saw the earthquake box on the ground. Testo ran for the box with Folks right behind him. Before Testo could reach the box, Folks grabbed him, and threw him to the ground. Testo's went face first, and when he hit the ground he laid about four feet away from the box. Testo went to get up, and Folks kicked him in his side. Testo fell down, and attempted to get up again. Folks kicked at Testo. Testo grabbed Folks' leg, and hit him in his stomach. Folks stooped over, and rammed Testo with his shoulders. Testo fell back, and grabbed Folks' shirt, pulling him to the ground. Testo laid on his back with his hands around Folks' neck. Folks was over top of Testo with both of his thumbs shoved into Testo's eyes.

The Connection, Zig-Zag and Valhalla moved around the perimeter of the island like foundation. "FOLKS!" yelled Zig-Zag. People were everywhere! Some were running, while others secured themselves behind cars or walls to watch in amazement what was going on. The Son of Lilith and his army moved from building top to building top following the action. Earth made her way through the crowd, and stood at the edge of the island that formed from the earthquake machine. She looked down, and saw that the pit looked almost bottomless. Earth looked over, and saw Folks and Testo fighting on the ground with their hands around each other's throats. Earth gasped! She then started running around the edge of the pit in order to try and get closer to Folks.

Testo kneed Folks in his stomach, and pushed Folks off of him. Testo jumped up, and grabbed the machine. Testo ran, Folks was right behind him. Testo reached back, and threw the machine. Folks kicked Testo from behind, and grabbed the machine just as it left Testo's fingers. Testo went flying forward, and fell off the side of the foundation and down into the enormous pit. Zig-Zag went running around the perimeter of the pit while shooting at Testo, who had now disappeared into the pit's abyss. There was nowhere for Folks to throw the earthquake machine. He looked around, and saw that buildings were still crumbling. Folks wrapped his arms around the box, and held it tightly against his chest. The vibrations force could not penetrate Folks' arms and chest. Folks, glowing a bright green, was shaking horribly from the box. His eyes started to roll to the back of his head. All of a sudden the shaking stopped, and Folks fell backwards. As he fell, the earthquake machine, which was now in pieces , also fell to the ground. Folks hit the pile of rocks hard, and stayed there. He was not glowing or moving. "NOOO!" yelled Zig-Zag. Valhalla fell to her knees in shock. The Connection's eyes were as wide as dinner plates, and had tears in them. Earth put her hand over her mouth. The crowd was silent. The Son of Lilith even had a hint of compassion in his face for Folks. Earth reached down, and grabbed a handful of dirt and small pebbles. Kneeling down, she threw the dirt from where she stood to the island that Folks laid on. A bridge of dirt and rock formed. Earth quickly ran across to Folks. She kneeled down at his head. Earth was in shock as she saw the blood coming out of Folks' mouth and nose. He was not glowing or moving. Earth picked up his head, and held it. "Remember, Folks, nothing is written in stone! Nothing is written in stone!" Earth said as she rocked slowly back and forth holding his head. Earth laid Folks' head down gently on the ground, and slowly stood up.

"ARGGH!" Zig-Zag screamed in pain. When Earth looked over at Zig-Zag he was on one knee, and bending over as he held his stomach. Just then large beautiful golden colored wings sprouted from Zig-Zag's back. Zig-Zag stood up, and was looking back at Earth. Earth stood there with tears in her eyes as Folks lay on the ground behind her. Earth looked down; a teardrop fell from her eye. Before it could hit the ground, a hand caught the tear. Earth turned around to see Folks standing there glowing a bright green. Earth put her hand over her mouth, as Folks wiped her tears from her face with his hand. Folks turned to see Zig-Zag with his golden wings. Zig-Zag let out a sigh of relief. "I knew it! He is the prodigy," the Connection whispered to himself. Valhalla stood there still in shook. Folks looked up at The Son of Lilith. The boy smiled at Folks, then said "TAP TAP!" The army came to attention. The boy's large wings sprouted, and he took off into the air followed by his army.

CHAPTER 14

The 24 Elders all stood on a balcony. They were all dressed in white. Down below were thousands of people who were also dressed in white. "This is truly a blessed day! We have been spared from destruction, and we will continue to move forward, thanks to fate," said Star 6, as he stood on the balcony, and spoke to the massive crowd.

The crowd cheered. "Thanks to fate!" said Zig-Zag in disgust.

"Let it go!" Valhalla said to Zig-Zag. Zig-Zag just shook his head.

"Where is that son of yours anyway?" Zig-Zag asked Valhalla.

"Oh now he's my son," said Valhalla.

"O.K.! Our son!" said Zig-Zag with a smile. "I think that he went to thank the person who really helped him through all of this," said Valhalla.

"Thank you, Valhalla," said Zig-Zag while looking up at The Elders on the balcony.

"You're more than welcome," whispered Valhalla as she looked up at Zig-Zag. Zig-Zag stood there with his golden wings spread far apart.

Folks came walking up to a field on 63rd and Baltimore Avenue. Inside of the field was a swing set on which Earth was sitting. Folks smiled, and walked over to her. Earth looked up at Folks, and smiled really big. Folks started to push Earth on the swing. "You really did a great job, Folks," said Earth. Folks just smiled. "You should spend some peaceful time with your mother and father now," said Earth.

"I don't know who they are. I never have," said Folks.

"You don't? You have been with them this whole time," said Earth, as

Folks pushed her on the swing. Folks couldn't believe what he just heard Earth say. He just stood there in shock. The swing came back, and gently crashed into Folks' legs. When Folks looked down, there were twelve red roses laying on the swing seat, and Earth was gone. Folks, still in shock, started to smile!